A Family

For

Hazel

BRIDES OF
PELICAN RAPIDS

By Linda Shenton

Matchett

A Family for Hazel
By Linda Shenton Matchett

Cover Design: Carpe Librum Book Design
Author photo by: Wes Matchett

ISBN-13: 978-1-7363256-7-4

Published by Shortwave Press

Chapter One

Her footsteps muffled on the plush carpet, Hazel Markham followed the maid to the parlor where her fate rested in the evil hands of her employer's son. Greedy, arrogant, odious, dishonest. She'd never run out of words to describe the horrid man. Her heart pounded in her ears as she approached the opulent room where Mrs. Agnew typically spent her afternoons entertaining her rich friends, but today was different. Hazel knew that as soon as she'd been summoned. Despite the woman's wealth, she never treated her servants with disdain. She would seek them out to discuss issues or instructions, so the command had to have come from James.

Hazel swallowed a sigh and straightened her spine. Something was definitely awry, but she would not appear as a scared kitten. She lifted her chin and entered the room. Moisture sprang out on her palms, and she clasped her hands together. The clock on the mantelpiece above the fireplace chimed the hour. Would she remember this moment the rest of her life?

Mrs. Agnew sat in her favorite blue floral Queen Anne chair. Her son stood behind her, his hand on her shoulder, and a triumphant smirk twisting his lips. His gray eyes studied Hazel like she was an insect under a microscope.

She pinned a smile on her face, her knees quaking. "How may I help you?"

"I'm very disappointed in you, Hazel." Mrs. Agnew's chin trembled. "You've been with me since your parents died, nearly eight years now. You worked your way up the ranks and earn a good salary. Your meals and lodging are provided. Why would you have a need to steal from me?"

"Steal from you?" Hazel gaped at the woman. "What is missing, and why do you think I took it?"

"Several pieces of my jewelry are gone, and you were seen going into my bedroom."

"That's a lie. I would never enter your room without Mrs. Waterford's permission. As housekeeper she's the only one allowed in your room."

"A thief and a liar." James crossed his arms. "I expected better from you, Miss Markham."

She shook her head. He was behind this. He'd probably stolen the pieces himself to cover a debt, and when his mother discovered the items were missing, he used the opportunity to punish Hazel for rebuffing his advances one too many times. His gambling problem was no secret among the servants. Or his expensive taste and love of alcohol.

"I haven't taken the jewelry." She held out her hands to Mrs. Agnew. "Please believe me. You have been generous and kind. I have no reason to steal."

"Well—"

"If you're telling the truth, you have nothing to worry about." James cut off his mother's words. "A search of your room should prove your case."

Hazel's heart fell. No doubt the search would unearth the items that he'd planted. Why did life have to be so hard? It had taken several years, but she'd adjusted to the loss of her parents: first her father, who died helping a family of slaves make their way to freedom, then her mother who withered away of a broken heart. A friend of the family had referred her to Mrs. Agnew, and the woman had agreed to add the grieving fourteen-year-old to her staff, creating a position.

She didn't mind working for a living, and enjoyed living among the other servants who enveloped her into their ranks. Then she bloomed into a young woman, catching James's lecherous eye. Thus far, she'd managed to evade his amorous attempts, but now she was paying the price.

"Fine." Hazel glared at James. "I'm sure you've stashed the jewelry among my things, so we best get to it."

"Hazel!" Mrs. Agnew pressed a gnarled hand to her chest. "You've no call to speak to James that way."

"My apologies, Mrs. Agnew."

"Mother, you wait here. I can take care of this." James patted his mother's arm, then gestured to the door. "Shall we?"

"Not without someone else present." Hazel pursed her lips. She didn't dare go into her room alone with the man. For too many reasons to count. "If you're mother isn't up to this, I'd like to call a maid."

His face darkened, and his eyes glinted. "Have it your way, but don't blame me when word of your thievery gets out." He walked to the wall and pulled the bell cord.

Moments later, one of the new housemaids appeared on the threshold. "Sir?"

"Please follow Miss Markham and me to her room. We need a witness to her misdeeds."

"Already finding me guilty, Mr. Agnew?"

"That will be enough, Hazel." Mrs. Agnew frowned. "We've done nothing to earn your disrespect."

Hazel pressed her lips together. Did the woman honestly not know about her son's activities? Did she truly think he was a shining example of manhood? Would she ever find out, or would he be able to hide his shameful behaviors forever? "Yes, ma'am."

Wide eyed, the maid stepped into the hallway and waited for Hazel and James to lead the way to the servants' wing of the massive house. They arrived at her room, and Hazel slipped the key from her pocket. With trembling hands, she unlocked the door, then entered and stood near the window, the maid beside her.

James shot her a sidelong glance, then marched to the bed where he lifted the mattress revealing his mother's sapphire necklace and matching earrings, an emerald bracelet and ring, and a diamond bracelet.

If the situation wasn't so dire, she would have laughed. He hadn't even made a pretense of searching.

The maid gasped.

Tears sprang to Hazel's eyes. She expected to see one piece, perhaps two, but the collection of gems glimmering in the light was worth a fortune. Maybe even more than she would ever earn in a lifetime. Was he perverted enough to want her jailed? She rubbed her damp palms on her skirt. "Are you going to have me arrested, James?"

"No, the items have been recovered, but you're fired, of course."

She schooled her features. "Of course."

"Don't pull your high-and-mighty act with me. You're nothing but a servant, a lowly maid. Maybe I should contact the police."

Pulling herself to her full height, she shrugged, exhibiting a calmness she didn't feel. "Whatever you think best, but they'll do a full investigation. Do you really want that?"

"I've no interest in dragging the family name through the newspaper. You've got one hour to pack your things and leave." He snapped his fingers at the maid. "You stay here and ensure she doesn't steal anything else."

The girl nodded, her face pale.

James snatched the items from the bed and strode from the room without a backward glance.

"Right. Let's get to it, shall we?" Hazel's shoulders slumped. "I'm sorry you've been put in this position."

"There's not need to apologize. I haven't been here long, but I know you didn't take those things."

The tightness eased in Hazel's chest. "You do?"

"Yes. I—" The maid licked her lips, then shook her head. "What can I do to help you?"

Hazel studied her for a long moment. Had James tried to force himself on the young woman? Was she afraid of what he would do if she stood up for Hazel? She rubbed her forehead. "Can you rustle up some newspapers to pack my mother's vase? I'll pay for them if necessary."

The young woman scurried out the door, and Hazel grabbed her satchel from the closet. She pulled her few belongings from the drawers and shoved them into the bag. Speed was more important than neatness. The sooner she got out of this house, the better.

Moments later, the maid returned and handed her a sheaf of newspapers. "These were in the trash bin."

"Perfect." Hazel tossed them on the bed, then laid the vase on top. As she rolled the paper around the urn, an advertisement framed in black and written in large letters caught her eye: Matrimonial Agency, Ella Milton, Proprietress. All inquiries confidential.

Had God just handed her the means to a fresh start? Could she marry a perfect stranger? What other choice did she have? In all probability, none.

A Family for Hazel

Chapter Two

"Dagmar, don't get too close to the water. You'll get your dress wet." Olav Kristensen cupped his hands around his mouth and shouted at his eight-year-old daughter who danced at the edge of Lake Michigan. The backs of his eyes pricked with tears as he watched the willowy, blonde-haired, blue-eyed girl who looked more like his wife with each passing day.

She rolled her eyes. "Yes, Papa."

Today marked the fifth anniversary since his beloved Sigrid's death, and he found himself on the shores of the huge lake where he'd proposed after coming home from the war. He'd told himself upon waking he would work through the day without a trip to their favorite place, but by midafternoon, memories had overwhelmed him, and he threw down his pen, shut the Bible he couldn't focus on, and hitched his horse to the wagon.

A warm breeze ruffled his hair and tugged at his jacket. He stripped the garment and slung it over his arm as he squinted at the sunlight, sparkling like diamonds on the waves. Dagmar's giggles floated toward him, and he smiled. Not only did she resemble her mother, but the silver tones of her laughter were nearly identical. Bittersweet, to be sure.

When would the sharp pain of his grief subside? When would he stop feeling like he'd lost a limb? Others remarried. Why couldn't he bring himself to find another mate? A woman to be a mother to his daughter and teach her how to be a lady.

"Papa, look what I found!" Hopping up and down, Dagmar waved her arm. The sun glistened on her flaxen hair, turning it almost white. "Come see."

Gulls shrieked and swooped overhead as if celebrating with her.

He blinked and ambled toward her, scolding himself as he walked. Live in the present, man. Sigrid is gone, and you've got a daughter who loves you. He swallowed a sigh and increased his pace. "Have you unearthed a treasure, little one?"

"*Ja.*" Her eyes glowed, and her cheeks were pink.

"Put on your bonnet, *søt hjerte.*" He frowned. Caught up in his thoughts, he'd failed to notice the head covering was dangling down her back, and now her face was getting burned. "You need to protect your skin."

She nodded and continued to inspect the glistening stone in her hand.

Olav chuckled and pulled the bonnet over her silky hair, then tied the strings. "Show me."

Holding out her hand, she gazed at the pebble. "It shines, Papa. Do you think it's gold?"

With his index finger, he stroked the chunk of rock, then picked it up and pretended to study it. "It is pretty, isn't it?"

"You didn't answer my question." Fists on her hips, she narrowed her eyes. "I'm not a little girl, Papa. You don't have to pretend."

"You are growing up, aren't you?" He handed her the stone, then squeezed her shoulder. "I don't think it's gold, but we could go to the jeweler and ask him."

"We can?" She closed his fist around the rock, then whirled away from him. "You hold that one, and I will look for more."

He pulled out his pocket watch. "A few more minutes, Dagmar, then we should go home so I can prepare supper. You're getting hungry, aren't you?"

She gave him a half-hearted wave.

Ever the explorer. Just like her mother.

"Olav."

With a final glance at his daughter to ensure she was safely away from the water, he turned. Three of the five elders from his church approached. His stomach clenched. What had caused them to search him out?

"Olav, a moment."

Forcing a smile, he lifted one hand in greeting. "Good afternoon, gentlemen. To what do I owe the pleasure?"

The tallest of the trio, Finn Calland, exchanged a glance with the other two, Johan Halderson and Lars Rendahl, then cleared his throat. "We've come to discuss an important matter."

"On my day off, and in front of my daughter?" Olav raised one eyebrow. "The topic must be grave."

The man had the grace to blush. "Ja, we think so."

"All right, but keep your voice down. Dagmar doesn't need to be privy to our conversation."

"Of course." Finn stuffed his hands in his pockets. "We are concerned that you have remained single for so long. It is not good for man to be alone."

"The Bible says that," Johan piped up.

"I'm well aware of the passage." Olav crossed his arms. "And I will admit it has been a challenge to raise Dagmar on my own, but I'm not ready to share my home with another woman."

"I understand. In addition to your grief, you feel guilty." Finn shrugged. "At least that's how it was with me after I lost Grethe. But Sigrid would want you to be happy, to have a full life. She wouldn't expect you to remain alone."

Olav blew out a loud breath. "I know, and even though my head agrees with you, my heart…"

"We're sorry for your loss, Olav, but it has been five years, long enough to grieve," Lars blurted.

"Who are you to tell me I should be finished with my grief?" Olav clenched his fists. "You who have been happily married to the same woman for thirty-five years."

"Well—"

"Get to the point, *gentlemen.*" Olav spoke through gritted teeth. "I'd like to get back to enjoying the day with my daughter."

"There's no need to get upset." Finn held up his hands in surrender. "But the elders have met and determined that you need to take a wife, whether you are ready or not. We want our church to be led by a married man. You need a partner to help with your ministry, and you can't visit our unmarried women by yourself."

"Is this an ultimatum?" Olav's pulse skittered. Would they force him out of the church if he didn't marry?

"We hesitate to use that term." Johan ducked his head.

"How long do I have?" Olav peeked toward the lake. Good, Dagmar was still out of hearing distance. "Do you have a deadline?"

Lars shuffled his foot in the dirt. "Four...no, six weeks."

Olav's breath exploded. "Impossible. I don't believe I should choose from the women at church, and I cannot find a suitable wife in less than two months."

"Miles found Rayne through a mail-order-bride agency. We suggest you do the same,"
Finn said.

"You've given this quite a bit of thought, haven't you?"

Their silence confirmed his suspicions.

"I'll find someone in eight weeks. Will that satisfy you?"

"Ja."

He pivoted on his heel and marched to the shoreline. "Dagmar. Time to go. Papa has to start supper." He frowned. And write an advertisement for a wife.

Chapter Three

Chatter filled the passenger car of the train as Hazel stared out the window. Odors of sweat and smoke assailed her as she mused over the last two weeks. Time had flown by as fast as the scenery outside the window. She'd telegrammed the matrimonial agency, and the owner required an interview, so she'd traveled to the woman's home in Minnesota. After being accepted as a client, she'd waited while Miss Milton determined which of her potential grooms would be a good fit for Hazel. She'd met several other brides-to-be, and they all had different reasons for using the agency.

Her stomach quivered. The man Miss Milton selected for Hazel was a preacher, and the irony wasn't lost on her. She was barely on speaking terms with God, and she was an accused thief, albeit innocent. The woman had shared Hazel's story with her prospective groom, a Norwegian who'd come to the country as a youngster, and he'd accepted her. Olav Kristensen. What a mouthful.

The man had a daughter. Hazel sighed and fiddled with the strap on her reticule. She knew nothing about raising children. Miss Milton assured her everything would work out, but Hazel wasn't so sure. Of course, her options were limited...no, nonexistent, so she was chugging her way to Wisconsin. She'd heard of the state, but had no idea where it was, so Miss Milton had to show her the location on a map.

Fortunately, the journey from Minnesota to Wisconsin wasn't nearly as long as the one had been from Pennsylvania to Minnesota. She had less time to fret about her new life...or prepare. Maybe she should reconsider her feud with God and pray about the situation. As if that would change anything.

She huffed out another sigh. The die was cast. She wouldn't go back on her word. Besides, one groom was as good as another, and a preacher would be a kind man. He would have to be. But what about his daughter? Would she despise Hazel for taking her mother's place? Not that the man would love Hazel as a wife. Perhaps she could explain that to the little girl. Would she understand? What did one do with an eight-year-old girl?

"Green Bay, next stop." The porter marched down the aisle. "Next stop, Green Bay."

Pulse tripping, Hazel clutched her bag to her chest. The train swayed and rattled as the brakes squealed. Smoke wafted past the windows, obscuring the view. The buzz of conversation swelled, and some of the passengers gathered their belongings in anticipation of disembarking. Steam hissed as the train lurched to a halt. Around her people rose and trooped toward the door.

This was it. She'd arrived. Willing her body to move, she grabbed her satchel from under the seat, then rose, and trudged toward the exit. She gripped the railing and climbed down the metal stairs. Her gaze swept the platform where porters unloaded trunks and bags amid the swarm of people.

Jostled from behind, she gasped. Tears sprang to her eyes. How would she know her prospective groom? She glanced at the watch pinned to her bodice. The train was thirty minutes early. Was the man here?

"Miss Markham?"

She whirled, and her eyes widened.

A blond man with startling green eyes stood with his hat in hand. A few inches taller than her five-foot-six-inch frame, he was broad-shouldered, looking more like one of the lumbermen in Pennsylvania than a preacher.

"Yes. Mr. Kristensen?"

"Ja." He bowed, his manner stiff and unyielding. "Thank you for coming. If you show me your bag, I will put it in the wagon."

She glanced at the collection of luggage, then gestured to a small brown trunk.

He lifted an eyebrow. "That is all you have?"

"Yes. Is that a problem?"

His cheeks flushed. "*Nei.*" He lifted the crate onto his shoulder as if it weighed nothing, then jerked his head to the line of conveyances along the curb. "The third wagon is mine. My daughter is with friend. I thought it best we meet alone for the first time."

"Of course."

Olav stowed her trunk, then helped her climb onto the wagon, his grip firm yet gentle.

She dropped onto the seat with a jolt, her hands tingling from his touch. She peeked at him out of the corner of her eye as he guided the horse out of the station. Expressionless, his profile looked to be etched in stone. Crow's feet bracketed his eyes above high cheekbones and full lips. His fair skin was tanned, and the sunlight glinted off the fine stubble on his chin. There hadn't been time to exchange photographs, but the Adonis sitting next to her was nothing like she'd expected.

"Miss Milton told me about you. About the...problem with your former employer. Is there anything you wish to tell me?"

"Such as?"

"Your side of the story."

"Miss Milton shared everything I told her. I was accused of stealing from Mrs. Agnew. Her jewelry was found under my mattress. I didn't put it there. I suspect her son did. He's...less than honorable. There's nothing more to say."

He studied her for a long moment, his peridot-colored eyes piercing her face.

She lifted her chin and refused to look away from the skepticism that clouded his face. Did he not believe her claims of innocence? Was she making a huge mistake by marrying this man?

Hands gripping the reins, Olav swallowed his disappointment. The woman seated next to him was nothing like Sigrid. Whereas his wife had been petite and slender, Miss Markham was a few inches shorter than him and rounded. Rather than gliding across the platform behind him as his wife would have done, his prospective bride marched beside him. Her brown hair was pretty enough. The color of cinnamon if he had to give it a name, but Sigrid's ash-blonde hair had been her crowning glory, her blue eyes reminiscent of Norway's icy glaciers, the antithesis of Miss Markham's chocolate-brown eyes.

She hunched into herself, her mouth turned down in a frown. He had a right to know about her background, and yet she seemed to resent his questions.

"If the charges weren't true, why didn't you stay in Pennsylvania? Surely, you could have obtained another position."

Her back stiffened, and she gave him a sidelong glance. "Is everything always black and white for you?"

"What do you mean?"

"I didn't get thrown in jail, so you figure I could simply go out and get another job." She snapped her fingers. "Because it's easy for a woman

19

to find employment, especially when she's been let go without a letter of reference from one of the most influential women in Waynesboro society. Of course, why didn't I think of that?"

His cheeks warmed. "Well—"

"My reputation is ruined. Torn to shreds by lies. No one would hire me. James made sure of that."

"I didn't realize."

"With a half day off per week, I had no marriage prospects either." The muscle in her jaw twitched. "And frankly, I got no support from my church."

"They—"

"Did nothing. In fact, most chose to believe the scuttlebutt and suggested I should repent of my wickedness."

His stomach hollowed. Where was her pastor during the situation? Church members had kicked her when she was down. Why had she agreed to marry him? Had Miss Milton pushed him off on her? Was he the only groom available?

Hazel cleared her throat, her face an impassive mask. "Why did you use an agency to find a wife? I would think there would be plenty of church ladies to fall in love with."

"I...uh...didn't think it was wise to choose from within my congregation. Besides, I'm not drawn to any of the few single women who attend."

She nodded. "That makes sense. Miss Milton said you were widowed five years ago. Why are you looking to get married now?"

He tightened his grip on the reins and stared at the dirt road ahead. He should have explained the situation to Miss Milton, then she could have told his prospective bride. Water under the bridge.

"*Are* you looking to get married?"

"Ja." He pulled on the traces and brought the wagon to a halt. Miss Markham deserved to be looked in the eye when he gave her his reason. He turned toward her. "I must wed in the next two months...well, six weeks now, to keep my job."

"What?" Her jaw hung slack.

"The elders came to me two weeks ago and said they were uncomfortable having a single man as their pastor. That it was time to put aside my grief." His voice broke, and he licked his lips. "Said if I wanted to remain at the church, I would have to marry."

Her eyebrows came together. "Isn't that a fine how-do-you-do? Rather arrogant to think you can stop grieving on their say-so."

The tightness in his chest eased. She understood, and she hadn't gotten angry at him. Instead, she took his side. Just like a wife would. He sent her a tentative smile. "Thank you for saying that."

"It seems Miss Milton knew what she was doing. I need a fresh start, and you need a partner in ministry. I'll do my best to be a good pastor's wife and mother to your little girl." She held up her hands. "Not that I expect to replace her real mother, but I can be her friend and help you raise her."

Olav slapped the reins on the horse's rump, and the wagon jerked forward. Hazel fell against him, and her hand grabbed his thigh. She pulled back as if scalded, her face flaming. Under the fabric of his pants, his skin sizzled as if he, too, had been burned. His body was betraying him. He could never develop feelings for this woman. Not while Sigrid still resided in his heart.

Chapter Four

Hazel stifled a yawn as she finished dressing. Olav had given her a tour of the town, then treated her to a late lunch at a small restaurant near the church. He had additional plans for their time, but she'd nearly fallen asleep over dessert, so he'd brought her to the boarding house where she'd be staying until they married.

She'd quickly unpacked, then fallen into bed, but tossed and turned most of the night, her mind swirling like autumn leaves on the ground. She pulled back the curtains and blinked at the murky sunlight. An occasional muffled shout seeped through the glass as pedestrians hurried along the crowded wooden sidewalks. Wagons rattled down the street.

Nothing like Waynesboro.

A sigh escaped, and she pressed her hand against her chest as she continued to watch the activity below. What had she gotten herself into? On the one hand, she was away from the whispering and gossip that pursued her day after day. Other than Olav, no one in Green Bay knew her history and wouldn't, thanks to James's desire to keep the incident out of the newspapers. More for his sake, of course, than hers. All she wanted was a fresh start, like she'd told Olav, and now she had one. She could make her life what she wanted it.

But on the other hand, she was marrying a stranger, a preacher whose job would put her under intense scrutiny from church members and townspeople alike. There would be expectations of her to act a certain way, do certain things, and hold certain attitudes. An onerous burden. She had yet to meet the elders who'd forced Olav to marry. Would they be as stiff necked and unbending as she imagined?

Most girls would be thrilled to snag such a handsome husband, and she certainly appreciated his good looks, but she was more interested in the man he was inside. She had her fill of elegant yet selfish, condescending men like James and his friends, who paraded through the house.

The afternoon had given her glimpses of Olav's character, and his tendency for snap judgments rankled her. By the time he dropped her off, she wondered if he truly believed she was innocent. And the lack of light in his eyes when they met seemed to say he didn't think her pretty. Why did men always set such importance in appearance? As a pastor, shouldn't Olav be different? Wasn't he supposed to be accepting of everyone? Especially the woman he was going to marry.

She turned from the window and checked her image in the mirror, then pinched her cheeks in an effort to add some color to her wan complexion. Normally fair skinned, the journey had been more fatiguing than she'd anticipated, leaving her face ashen. Half-moon-shaped dark smudges hung below her eyes: a nondescript brown, that matched her unremarkable brown hair and stuck out in a city full of Scandinavians with icy-blonde hair and blue eyes.

"Stop it." Hazel shook her finger at her reflection. "Comparison is a joy killer. Find the blessings in this situation."

A knock sounded, and she jumped. "Just a moment."

"Mr. Kristensen is here." The unfamiliar voice must belong to one of her fellow boarders.

"I'll be right there."

"Yes, miss. I'll let him know." Footsteps faded.

With a deep breath, Hazel smoothed her skirts, then snatched her reticule and shawl from the bed. She took a final glance around the room before leaving and locking the door. Her pulse skittered like an unbroken horse trying to lose its rider. She pinned on a smile and descended to the lobby.

Hat in one hand, Olav stood with the other hand on the shoulder of a lithe, blonde girl wearing a broad grin. He nodded, his face expressionless. Did the man have no feelings whatsoever?

"Are you my new mama," the child blurted.

Hazel's heart swelled. No matter what she thought of Olav, she would love this little girl as her own. "That's what your daddy and I are trying to figure out." She crouched in front of the child, so they could be eye level. "But you and me are going to be great friends. Your name is Dagmar. Is that what you like to be called?"

"Papa sometimes calls me Dagie, but I like Dagmar."

"Then that is what I shall call you. And you may call me Miss Hazel. Will that be all right? Miss Markham seems so formal between friends, don't you think?"

Dagmar bounced on her heels. "I like you, Miss Hazel."

"And I like you, too." Tears filled her eyes, and she blinked them away. The little girl's unconditional, unrestrained acceptance was a balm to Hazel's soul. She rose and slipped her hand into Dagmar's. "What is on the agenda today?"

"Agenda?" Dagmar cocked her head. "I don't know that word."

"It means plan or list." Hazel slanted a glance at Olav. "What do you and your papa want to do today?"

"I have a meeting with the elders at church, so I thought you and Dagmar could spend time at the house until I'm done." His hands tightened on the brim of his hat. "Afterwards, we can finish the tour of Green Bay and perhaps have a picnic by the water. Is that acceptable to you?"

The tension seeped from her back, and she nodded. "Absolutely. You take as long as you need. Dagmar and I will get along famously."

"Thank you." The corner of his mouth lifted. "Frankly, I'd rather be with you two, but I've already delayed this meeting twice. A third time wouldn't go down too well."

"And best to get it over with." She gestured to the door. "Does Dagmar know the way home? If so, there's no need for you to take us."

Dagmar giggled. "I know exactly where we live. Why would you ask that?"

Cheeks burning, Hazel shrugged. "Because I've never had a friend your age."

"Oh." The child flipped her platinum-blonde hair. "Well, eight-year-old girls know a lot. Isn't that right, Papa?"

He chuckled. "Ja. Sometimes too smart for their own good."

Hazel swallowed a gasp. Good looking in repose and even when frowning, Olav was gorgeous when he smiled. His face shone as if lit from within, and his eyes sparkled, snapping with humor and love for his daughter. His teeth flashed white and bright against his tanned face. She swallowed and held out her hand to Dagmar. "We should let your father get to his meeting."

Dagmar grabbed her fingers and waved at Olav with her other hand. "Bye, Papa. Try not to stay too long."

Ruffling her hair, he nodded, then pivoted and headed toward the church.

With a skip in her step, Dagmar led Hazel to the house, a small, whitewashed cabin with a tiny porch on which two rockers sat side by side. The door was painted a buttery-yellow color. They went inside, and Hazel froze. A large photograph of a fair-haired woman hung above the fireplace. The wall above the couch was graced with a blue-and-white, log-cabin-patterned quilt. Another quilt was draped over an upholstered chair in the corner. Quilted placemats brightened the kitchen table. A large trunk sat under the window. Were there more quilts inside?

"Your mother liked to sew?" Hazel's gaze continued to ricochet around the space.

"Ja." Dagmar pointed to the picture. "That's her, but I have a hard time remembering her. I was only three when she died."

"Then it's good your father has the portrait." Hazel pressed her lips together. Would she have to live under the woman's watchful gaze for the rest of her life?

Chapter Five

The crisp scent of soap and lavender water wafted toward him from Hazel as Olav guided the wagon through the streets of Green Bay. His stomach clenched, and he forced his attention to the road. Dagmar sat in the back chattering to her rag doll.

His meeting with the elders had dragged on for an hour and had proceeded about as expected. They'd been pleased to hear that his bride-to-be had arrived, but spent an enormous amount of time interrogating him about her background and religious beliefs. They seemed irritated he could answer very little about both and indicated he needed to find out. His blood boiling, he'd risen and assured them he was capable of determining whether the woman was acceptable.

He cast a sidelong glance at her and sighed. She sat with her hands clasped in her lap, her neck swiveling as she surveyed the buildings and pedestrians. The few times they'd attempted conversation had been stilted and awkward. Would their interaction become less labored as time passed? They seemed to have nothing in common. Miss Milton assured him they were suited, but how could she possibly know that?

Several turns later, they arrived at the bay, and Hazel gasped. He smiled. He'd had the same reaction the first time he'd seen the beautiful body of water.

Pulling on the traces, he stopped the wagon, then set the brake. "What do you think of our bay?"

"It's so vast." She blinked and gestured toward the horizon. "It's almost like the ocean."

"Ja." He nodded. "There are no waves, but the lake does experience tides, although not as extreme as the sea."

Her eyes sparkled in the sunlight, and her lips curved. "Thank you for showing me. This is lovely." She twisted in the seat to look behind her. "How far are we from your house? I'm afraid I'm a bit disoriented. Is this walking distance?"

"I'd prefer you and Dagmar didn't come here alone." He gestured across the lake. "Even though this area is peaceful, we're not far from the harbor which is teeming with workers. Most are upstanding men, but not all can be trusted." He frowned. "In fact, I'd prefer it if you didn't wander the streets by yourself, even after you become familiar with where the shops are."

"Oh." She shuddered. "Is the city dangerous?"

"It can be, but you should be safe if you take the right precautions."

"I understand."

He clicked his teeth and slapped the reins on the horse's rump, and the wagon lurched forward. She continued to crane her neck and shift in the seat as she took in the activity. Several minutes later, they reached the docks. Smoke belched from the chimneys at the iron furnace company overlooking the mouth of the Fox River. Sailing vessels and steamboats made their way in and out of the harbor. Shouts peppered the clanging and banging, and men rushed back and forth between the watercraft and the pier. In the distance, a train whistle shrieked.

"I've never seen anything like this in my life." Her eyes bulged as she turned toward him. "Where do the ships come from? Where are they going?"

"Chicago and New York mostly." He gestured to a stack of railroad ties. "Wisconsin is known for its forests. Lumber, barrels, shingles, and railroad ties are the primary products, but the state lost a lot of business three years ago because of the Peshtigo fire. Flames took out over a million acres, and more than a thousand people died."

"How sad."

"Folks here are resilient, and the ports are nearly as busy as they once were." He guided the wagon onto the main road, and the noise faded behind them. After a glance at Dagmar to see if she was listening, he cleared his throat. "Hazel, I want you to know I appreciate you uprooting yourself to be my bride, but before we marry, we must decide if we are compatible."

She stiffened, and one of her eyebrows lifted. "I thought Miss Milton determined that already."

"From what I understand, she conducts a background check of sorts, but that doesn't guarantee we'll be suited."

"Fair enough." Back ramrod straight, she crossed her arms. "What would you like to know?"

He swallowed a sigh. He'd obviously offended her. Was she always so easily vexed? "As a pastor, it is important for my wife to hold to the same tenets as I do. I know you are believer, but what church are you affiliated with?"

She narrowed her eyes. "Are labels important to you, Olav? What does it matter if I'm Baptist, Methodist, or Lutheran? Will you reject me if I don't give you the right answer?"

"Denominations came about because of differences in beliefs." He shrugged. "What would the church think if we didn't agree?"

"Is it really any of their business?" She frowned. "I don't mean to be obstinate, but isn't our marriage none of their business?"

"Unfortunately, no. That is one thing I learned early in my ministry." He stopped the wagon in front of a grassy area that overlooked the lake. "Churches feel they have a say-so in my life, and by association, in yours. I will not let them in our personal lives, but they have a right to know how we believe."

"Fine." She huffed out a breath and tucked a stray hair behind her ear. "I went to church from the time I was a baby, but didn't come to know the Lord until I was twelve years old. That's when I realized I needed Him, that I was a sinner, and that I could only go to heaven if I believed that Jesus died and rose for me." A shimmer of tears formed in her eyes. "After my parents died, I turned away because I was angry at Him for letting that happen. Mrs. Agnew took me in and was kind. Eventually, I stopped blaming God, and my faith was restored. My initial reaction after being falsely accused of stealing my employer's jewelry was to grumble that He'd let it happen, but I've come to terms that even if He did, He must have some plan for good." She tilted her head. "Do I measure up, or should I pack my bags?"

"I didn't mean for this to feel like an interrogation." His face heated. "I...uh...just think it's important that we understand each other and are of like mind."

"I agree, but you're simply marrying me to keep your job. How compatible do we need to be?"

Olav pressed his lips together. Her bluntness was nothing like Sigrid's sweet and gentle nature. What had he gotten himself into? More importantly, how could he be irritated and attracted at the same time?

A Family for Hazel

Chapter Six

Late afternoon sun cast shadows over the church, and Hazel squinted across the yard at the crowd milling around the food tables. Dagmar sat beside her, legs swinging on the hard, wooden bench. Women in brightly colored dresses mingled with the men in dark pants and crisp white shirts. Laughter and shouts ringing, children darted among the adults.

Olav trotted toward her, a smile lighting his face. They'd come to an awkward truce after their tour of the city, but today they'd both managed to put aside their hesitancy and regaled in the joy and fun of the festival. He waved as he approached, his skin flushed and damp from the heat of the day. "How do you like your first experience with Norwegian food?"

She wrinkled her nose. "Most of it is delicious, but I haven't developed a taste for pickled herring or beets."

He chuckled and leaned close. "I haven't either, but I love lutefisk. Did you try some?"

"Yes, but I must admit the desserts are my favorite." Her pulse thrummed at his proximity. How could he affect her after only a few days?

"I...uh...will learn how to make your native dishes, but you must be patient."

"Vanessa Andersen married into our community. You should get to know her. She's from somewhere in the south." He wiggled his eyebrows. "She can probably give you insight in our ways...the good and the bad."

With a giggle, Hazel nodded. "I'll be sure to hunt her down."

"Did Dagmar tell you about the festival and why we celebrate?" He ruffled his daughter's hair. "She loves to recite the history of our forebears."

"We keep getting interrupted by ladies who want to meet Hazel." Dagmar frowned and gestured to Hazel's half-filled plate. "They ask lots of questions, and she hasn't had time to eat."

"It's okay, honey," Hazel said. "They're just curious."

"Nosy is more like it."

"Dagmar!" Olav frowned. "That's not a very nice thing to say."

She shrugged. "It's true, and you know it."

Hazel swallowed a grin. The child was right. Most of the women present had paraded past, asking pointed questions about Hazel and her family. A bug under a glass would receive less attention. "We are alone now, so why don't you tell me about the festival, and I will finish my food."

Straightening her spine, Dagmar flicked her blonde hair over her shoulder, then took a deep breath. "Papa is named after King Olaf, who was king more than eight hundred years ago. In Norway, they didn't believe in God until Olaf brought news of Him to the country. There were lots of little kings, but he was over them. They listened to him for a while, but then they decided they didn't want him anymore and made him leave. He went to Sweden for a couple of years, but he wanted to be king again and came back with a great army, but he was killed."

"Well, that's quite a story. Is July twenty-ninth his birthday? Is that why you celebrate on this day?"

Dagmar shook her head. "No, it is the day he died. The Catholics...cannoned...cann... made him a saint."

"Canonized." Hazel sipped from her cup. "A big word, isn't it?" She peeked at Olav from under her bangs. Did he believe in saints? Was that part of the Lutheran beliefs? Her tiny church in Waynesboro would be appalled if she joined a denomination that touted saints. Maybe she should turn the tables on the elders and quiz them. But that was for another day. Today was about fun, and fortunately, she didn't have to force herself to appear as if she were having a good time.

Olav lowered himself beside her, his warmth seeping through her skirts when his leg pressed against hers, and she nearly dropped her plate. Her stomach quivered. She laid down her fork. "I hate to waste food, but that's all I can eat."

He took the plate, their fingers grazing. "I always have room for more."

Dagmar rolled her eyes. "Papa is never full."

Hazel snickered and wiped her damp hand on her napkin. "I'll remember that."

"Hey, I'm right here, you know." The corner of his mouth lifted in a crooked smile, and he nudged her shoulder. "Try not to talk about me as if I can't hear you."

The noise around them faded away as she stared into his eyes, the color of new grass in the spring. His teasing attitude was a side she hadn't seen since arriving. He'd shed his wariness and was not as guarded as he'd been. Had he accepted her, or was he simply caught up in the day's festivities? Time would tell, but there wasn't much left. The wedding loomed just weeks away.

Miles hollered to Olav from behind the food tables. He broke his gaze with Hazel and blinked as he lifted his hand in response. He'd been close enough to see the gold flecks in her chocolate-brown eyes. Eyes that snapped with intelligence and some other emotion he couldn't pinpoint.

Wearing blue jeans and black cowboy boots, his friend trotted toward him. Despite the man's wealth, he and his wife, Vanessa, were two of the most down to earth people Olav knew. He'd floundered when he first arrived in the town, and they'd enveloped him as if he were family, and never let go. They'd celebrated Dagmar's birth and mourned Sigrid's death. Since then, Miles had been his confidante, encourager, and voice of reason. And he was the reason Hazel was in Green Bay as his future bride.

She tensed, her fingers clutching her skirts. Why was the woman so skittish?

Dagmar hopped off the bench and flung herself against Miles. He laughed and picked her up, then swung her in a circle. Her giggles rang like silver bells.

"You're getting too big for *Onkel* Miles." Olav smiled. "And he's getting too old."

"Nonsense." Miles set her down, then stroked her cheek with his finger. He bowed at Hazel. "What do you think of our little festival?"

"It's wonderful." She ducked her head. "Learning about your culture and history is fascinating. I'm abashed to say I don't know much about Norway or those who emigrated from Norway to America."

Olav gave her a dismissive wave. "No reason to be embarrassed." He pursed his lips. He'd been stunned by the number of questions she'd asked. He knew more about America before he'd come than she knew about Norway. How was that possible? Should he reconsider marrying a non-Norwegian woman? What would it be like to live out the rest of his life with a person of different heritage? How would her background affect Dagmar?

"How long has your family been in America?" Miles stuffed his hands in his pockets and rocked on his heels. "Do you have a single ancestry?"

"We have been here since before the Revolution with England, but my parents and grandparents didn't talk much about our history."

"A shame you don't know," blurted Olav.

Miles shook his head. "She is a true American, blending cultures and histories like a tapestry."

Dagmar crawled onto the bench and slipped her hand into Hazel's, then snuggled against her shoulder. "I'm tired, Papa, and I ate too much."

He brushed a stray hair from her forehead. In mere days, his daughter seemed to have bonded with his future bride. At eight years old, heritage and ancestry were of no interest to Dagmar. Hazel had been sweet and gentle with the girl, showering her with affection. That was all that mattered to the child.

What would Sigrid think of Hazel? Would she be glad he'd found someone to assuage his loneliness and help raise their daughter? Would she take exception to his taking a non-Norwegian as his wife? Would she believe Hazel's claims of innocence, or would she delve further into the situation to determine its veracity? As she lay on her bed, health failing, she insisted he remarry, but they hadn't talked about specifics. He was too busy not believing she was going to die. His heart shattered as he'd held her hand and agreed to everything she said just to make her feel better.

He caught Miles staring at him, his brow pulled together. Had his friend said something he didn't hear because of his musings? From the corner of his eye, he could see Hazel study him as well. He *had* missed something, and after their conversation in the wagon, he was probably on thin ice with her. Being widowed was lonely, but in some ways it was much easier than navigating a relationship with a woman he barely knew.

A Family for Hazel

Chapter Seven

Scissors tight in her hand, Hazel cut out crude figures from the flannel in her lap in preparation for the week's classes. Despite her lack of experience with children, she'd agreed to help Olav with his summer Bible school that started in three days. He'd come up with the idea when he first arrived, and each year the number of kids increased. He expected more than one hundred little ones for this session.

Her mouth dried. Was her participation another test? When he asked for her help, he indicated she could turn him down, but he looked at her with such hope, she couldn't bring herself to refuse. He assured her that one of the church ladies would be with her, but was working with a stranger who watched her every move better or worse than floundering alone?

She finished with the fabric and tucked the pieces into a small bag that she pinned to the flannel-covered board. Using the prop would give her something to do with her hands as she explained the story of Noah and his ark. How had Mrs. Noah felt about her husband's call to build a ship large enough to fill with animals? The poor woman was stuck inside the vessel for nearly a year. What had gone through her mind during the ordeal? Perhaps she deserved to be talked about too.

Pushing to her feet, Hazel wandered to the front of the room where Olav painted on a large banner. Every other man she knew would have considered the task women's work, but he'd thrown himself into the project with abandon, sketching the design with charcoal before putting brush to the canvas.

Hair disheveled and spiked, he looked up as she approached. A smudge of green paint marred his left cheek, and another covered his chin. "Please say you've come to help me. Whitewashing my house was easier than this."

Hazel giggled and picked up a rag and dipped the cloth in the small cup of water nearby. Without thinking, she started to rub the spot from his jaw.

Eyes riveted on her face, he stilled, his body taut.

Sunlight through the windows caused the faint golden-brown stubble on his face to glisten against his tanned skin. Her face warmed, and she dropped the rag. "I-I'm sorry. That was very forward. Forgive me." She fiddled with a paint brush on the table.

He studied her for a long moment, his face flushed, then bent to retrieve the abandoned cloth. He straightened and gave her a crooked grin. "Do I have more paint on me than the project?"

Heart pounding, she shrugged. It seemed her husband-to-be was a gentleman, easing her discomfort by acting like what she'd done hadn't occurred.. "Not quite. But...uh...you do have a bit on your chin."

"Do you want to finish what you started?" He held out the scrap. "Or should we wait until I've completed the job, because this won't be the last of the paint on me."

With bated breath, she took the fabric and rubbed the last of the color from his face, her fingers tingling even though the material separated her skin from his. She'd never been this close to a man before, and his proximity was disconcerting. "Done." Her voice trembled in her ears. Had he heard the wobble? She cleared her throat, then pinned on a smile. She needed to get a grip. "I'd be happy to finish the banner if you have other chores."

His peridot-colored eyes lit up, and he rubbed his hands together. "I do need to set up the classrooms. Do you have a preference how yours is arranged?"

"No...well...actually, the children might like to sit on the floor. Perhaps make the room seems less like regular school and more like camp or an adventure."

"Brilliant." He nudged her shoulder. "You're much better at this than you think."

Hazel's knees quivered. One minute she was at odds with Olav, and the next she was swooning like a schoolgirl. His gentle teasing and the respect with which he treated her struck a chord in her heart. Were her feelings attraction or loneliness?

Olav winked at Hazel, and her face reddened. She was a gentle soul who embarrassed easily, and despite their rocky start, she seemed anxious to fit in and support him. Her ideas about how to teach the various Bible stories he wanted covered during the week were creative and sure to engage the children.

She'd looked horrified when he'd asked her to join the team as one of the teachers, stammering that she had no experience whatsoever with children, and she'd be better working behind the scenes. After he assured her she'd have a partner and that the curriculum was already planned, she'd relaxed, but still seemed dubious about her success. She'd arrived this morning armed with propositions and plans that she'd discussed with Dagmar who loved every suggestion.

He realized he was still staring, and he slid his gaze to the banner lying on the table. "It...uh...seems as if you have everything in hand, so I'll head to the classrooms."

She nodded, and he caught the expression of relief that danced across her face as she turned to the table.

His stomach hollowed as he strode from the room. Did she find him distasteful? Or did he make her nervous? Their conversations were alternately enlightening and awkward. If he delved too deeply into her past, she got wide-eyed and jumpy. Were her employer's allegations of stealing true, and she was afraid of being found out? Or had the incident created distrust with everyone?

Her knowledge of the Bible was impressive, more in-depth than some of the men in the church. Had her parents seen to her education or had she studied on her own? She'd talked of her anger at God after their deaths, but perhaps her journey back to faith had caused her to probe the scriptures for answers.

After pushing the chairs to the edge of the room, he swept the dirt from the floor, then shook his head. Too spartan. He snapped his fingers. Quilts would make the space more welcoming. He could cover the floor and the walls, but where to get the comforters? He twisted his lips. There were two trunks in the attic filled with Sigrid's work. He'd shoved them there after her death. Should he keep them hidden away or risk tearing open the wound of her loss seeing the items she'd crafted?

He rubbed his chest. Would the ache of her absence ever go away? Would he ever care for Hazel as a man does for a wife? He'd prayed for a mate, and God had provided Miss Milton's agency. Surely, Hazel was His choice for him and Dagmar, and He wouldn't have done so if she was guilty of a crime. Would He?

She wasn't as pretty as Sigrid, but he hadn't expected to find another woman as beautiful. She treated his daughter with kindness and affection and had drawn alongside him in his work. Her spirit was gracious, and she was intelligent with a quick wit. Sigrid had been more staid, quietly going about her chores. When she was with Dagmar, Hazel laughed with abandon, and he smiled at the memory of the sound.

Olav gulped. There were numerous verses in the Bible reprimanding the desire for beauty over character. "Forgive me, Lord. My yearning for a fine-looking wife is a sin. I'm trying to impress others with her appearance when I should be proud of her humble and compassionate personality." He grimaced. For all he knew, she didn't find him attractive either.

Chapter Eight

The bread dough tightened under his hands as Olav kneaded the mass, the earthy smell of the yeast filling his nostrils. Nearby, Hazel instructed Dagmar how to measure the ingredients for cookies. Humidity clung to the air inside the kitchen as dappled sunlight filtered through the window to mingle with the warmth from the oven. He pressed his sleeve to his forehead to absorb the moisture that had formed. He would no longer take meal preparation for granted.

Hazel excused herself to Dagmar and came over to where he was working. She poked the lump, then smiled. "Well done. We'll make a baker of you yet."

His chest swelled. Her praise made him feel like a schoolboy who'd won a prize. "I had a good teacher."

Her cheeks pinked. "The next step is to lay a damp cloth over it while it rises. Then we'll punch it down and form it into a loaf." She checked the watch on her bodice. "It may take an hour or so." She picked up the bowl.

"I'll wash up." He took the dish and put it in the sink. "If I'm to learn, I have to perform all the steps."

Surprise lightened her eyes. "Okay. I'll finish with Dagmar. She's doing a good job with the cookies. We'll be able to have them for dessert."

"Or hor d'oeuvres." He grinned and grabbed a spoon from the counter.

She snatched the utensil from him, with a giggle. "Don't you dare."

Yanking the spoon from her, he reached around her to dig into the cookie dough.

Dagmar slapped his hand. "Papa, not yet."

He jumped back. Frowning in mock anger, he said, "Daughter, it's not right to hit your father, even if he's misbehaving." He swung around toward Hazel. "Tell her to show a little respect."

She guffawed, then covered her mouth with one hand, her eyes dancing. She shook her head.

"You're telling me I deserved that?" Unable to keep up the farce, he snickered, then blossomed into a full-fledged laugh. He wrapped his arms around his middle as the three of them roared with amusement.

"Papa, I like when you help with the cooking."

"I do, too, baby girl." He winked at her, then took a deep breath. He hadn't worked in the kitchen with Sigrid. She'd never asked for assistance, and he'd never offered. She had her chores, and he had his. Society dictated the delineation of responsibilities. How much joy had he missed by leaving her to her own devices?

He glanced at Hazel, who leaned against the table, myriad emotions fighting for supremacy on her face.

She met his eyes, and her lips curved. "You know the cookies will be late coming out of the oven because of your shenanigans."

"Who says we have to eat on schedule?" Olav pumped water into the sink to wash the bread-making items. "What is for lunch, anyway?"

"I'm going to fry up your leftover steak and potatoes into hash. You also have some lovely green beans in the larder."

His mouth watered. "Sounds delicious."

"It's not exactly haute cuisine, but it will be filling." She lowered her eyes. "We haven't discussed your food likes and dislikes, and what...uh...your wife used to make."

"Papa eats everything," Dagmar piped up. "He especially likes sweets."

"Are you going to tell Hazel all of Papa's secrets?"

"Everyone knows, even the ladies at church."

Hazel lifted her eyebrow and pushed away from the counter, a saucy smile on her face. "So much for secrets." She gestured toward the living room. "Now, you've *helped* enough. Why don't you work on a sermon or something? Dagmar and I will finish the baking and get lunch going."

He crowded her and made a show of towering over her. He tweaked her nose. "What if I want to help some more?" He'd never teased

Sigrid like this. Their relationship had been placid, sedate. His mind groped for the right word.

Backing up, she pressed her hands against his chest.

Warmth pierced his skin through his shirt, and he clamped his lips together against the gasp that bubbled up. Sigrid had been the wife of his youth, and they'd had a good marriage. But he was a grown man now, and things were different with Hazel, even after the short time since her arrival.

"Miss Hazel, did you really come through the mail?"

They both swung their gaze toward Dagmar. He cocked his head. "What? Where did you hear that?"

"At church, Mrs. Prytz said that Papa made a mail order."

Hazel shook her head. "Some people call women like me who either answer newspaper advertisements or use a matrimonial agency mail-order brides. But the postman doesn't deliver us. We come by train or stagecoach."

"Oh." She put one finger to her chin. "But—"

"What have I told you about eavesdropping in adult conversations?"

"But I wasn't. She asked if Miss Hazel was a friend of the family. She had other questions, too."

"I'll bet." Olav frowned. The woman was a known gossip. He should have guessed she'd ply Dagmar for information. He'd keep his daughter closer in the days ahead.

"When are you going to get married? If Miss Hazel is to be my new mama, shouldn't you have a wedding. I love weddings."

He peeked at Hazel, whose face flamed. She obviously wasn't used to the probing and difficult questions from eight-year-old girls. He crossed his arms with a chuckle. "And how many weddings have you attended?"

"Just one." She looked wistful. "But it was wonderful. Miss Rasch was beautiful. She looked so happy. She kind of glowed, don't you think?"

"All brides are beautiful. Getting married is one of the best days of their lives."

Dagmar slipped her hand into Hazel's. "I'm glad you're going to be my mama. I like you."

"I like you, too." She stroked his daughter's hand. "I told you we were going to be great friends."

"Mrs. Prytz said you're a little old to be a bride. Is that true? How can someone be too old to get married?"

"Goodness." Hazel's hand flew to her throat. "This Mrs. Prytz has a lot to say, doesn't she."

"I'm afraid so." Olav tamped down his anger. He would speak to the woman the first chance he got. "Dagmar, Hazel is not too old, and it's impolite to ask about a woman's age. Now, don't you have cookies to finish?"

"Yes, Papa." She tugged at Hazel's skirt. "When you and Papa get married, I hope I get a sister. It would be fun to have a sister."

Olav gaped at Dagmar and fought the urge to crawl under the table.

Chapter Nine

Hazel pressed the fabric-cut-out of the dove onto the flannel board as she finished the story about Noah and his ark. Movement across the churchyard caught her attention, and she shielded her eyes as she squinted against the glare. Olav sat cross-legged on the ground surrounded by boys and girls around Dagmar's age. Were they asking difficult and intrusive questions as the child had done two days ago in the kitchen?

Her cheeks warmed at the memory. Fortunately, Dagmar hadn't pushed for an answer when she declared her desire for a sister, but the words had hung in the air long after she voiced them. Olav had studiously avoided looking at Hazel throughout dinner, and the conversation had been stilted. Was he embarrassed or disgusted at the thought of having children with her?

His face was animated, and he stretched his arms as he talked to the group. His shirt strained against the muscles in his back. With broad shoulders that tapered to his waist, brawny arms, tanned face, he didn't look like any preacher she had ever seen. Granted, she'd only known two in her life, but neither had swung a hammer to help a friend or repaired fences. Neither was built like her prospective groom.

The group laughed as one, and her stomach quivered. He deserved more kids. He was good with them, interacting at their level without speaking down to them. Dagmar sat at the edge of the circle, head down as she fiddled with her boot laces. Her eyebrows were drawn together, and she periodically looked up long enough to glare at her father. What had happened to cause the little girl's sour mood?

Hazel clapped her hands, then nodded toward Mrs. Gjerstad, who had volunteered to work with her. "All right, children. Story time is over, so let's stretch our legs and work out the wiggles before our next activity. How does that sound?"

Giggling and talking, they leapt up and began to mill around.

She rose and grabbed Erik, the most rambunctious of them. "We're going to play follow the leader, and Erik is the leader, so you need to do everything he does." Her gaze went to Mrs. Gjerstad, and she mouthed, "I'll be back in a trice."

The woman nodded and corralled the kids behind Erik. They jostled each other to line up as Hazel traipsed across the yard. Olav flashed her a look, and she pointed to Dagmar and then herself. He dipped his head in acknowledgment, and she squatted beside the girl. "Do you mind giving me some assistance," Hazel whispered. "Mrs. Gjerstad and I have more children than we can handle."

Dagmar scrambled to her feet and headed toward Mrs. Gjerstad.

"I'll take that as a yes." Hazel grinned at Olav, who sent her a grateful smile. Her pulse hummed, and she forced herself to turn back to her task. My, but he was good looking. With a deep breath, she trotted to Dagmar and slipped her arm around the little girl's shoulder. "Before we do, I thought we could grab some water and chat. How does that sound?"

She shrugged and scuffed her feet in the dirt.

"Did something upset you, honey? Is there anything you want to tell me?" Hazel led her to the table where she filled a cup with water from one of the pitchers. She handed the drinking vessel to Dagmar, then poured one for herself. She took a long draft, and the tepid liquid soothed her dry throat. What did she know about counseling a troubled youngster?

Gesturing to a nearby set of chairs, she sat down, and Dagmar dropped beside her with a sigh. Hazel cradled the cup in her palms. "My papa wasn't a preacher, but he was a leader among men, and sometimes it was hard to be his daughter. Because of who he was, people had expectations about me that weren't always fair. There were days I wanted to be in a different family."

A smile bloomed on Dagmar's face. "Yes. Sometimes I wish he wasn't the pastor. Is that a bad thing? Will God punish me for thinking that?"

"Not at all." Hazel sipped her drink. "God wants us to be honest with Him about how we feel, especially when we are hurting."

"I'm the only one without a mother." Dagmar's chin trembled. "They don't understand."

"You're right, but until someone walks that road, they can't." She put her cup on the ground, then reached for Dagmar's hand. "I know exactly how you're feeling. I lost my mother, and it left a hole in my heart."

"Were you little like me when your mama died?"

"No, I was fifteen, but no matter how old you are, it hurts." She stroked Dagmar's fingers. "You can talk to me about your pain, but more importantly you can pray about how you feel. Anytime of the day or night, God is listening. He will help the hurt go away." Hazel bolted upright. She should have been doing that very thing. Instead, she moped and complained to herself. She could take her troubles to the Lord and tell Him how disappointed she was that Olav would never love her as a wife because of his grief. She had God's love, and she would learn to make that enough.

Hazel's words wafted toward him on the breeze as he watched her with Dagmar. What a fool he'd been. He'd been so enveloped in his own loss, he hadn't thought about how Sigrid's death affected his daughter. That she would experience a void in her life. He thought he'd successfully been both mother and father to her. Her conversation with Hazel told him how he'd failed.

His heart clenched, and he squelched the desire to grab his little girl into a fierce hug and apologize to her. Should he consider giving up the church? His ministry? To hear her tell it, she was suffering being the child of a pastor. He was used to the scrutiny of being in the pulpit, of having his every action and word examined, analyzed, and sometimes torn apart. But he'd never thought that Dagmar was subjected to the same behaviors. He'd been blind.

And Hazel had also endured the deaths of her parents. Miss Milton from the matrimonial agency had informed him that she was an orphan, but he'd taken the information in stride, assuming the misfortune occurred during her adulthood, as if that made the bereavement less difficult.

He was an insensitive oaf. What could he do to make it up to them?

"Your papa needs to know how you feel, honey," Hazel said. "He understands more than you think he does."

"I don't want to make him sad by talking about Mama."

"Being sad is okay, but perhaps sorting through your memories together will make you both a little less so."

Olav's breath whooshed out of him. Hazel's insight and wisdom were spot on.

"Pastor?"

He blinked, and his face flamed. Encircling him on the ground, the children stared at him. Roy, the closest little boy, tugged at Olav's sleeve. "Pastor," he repeated. "Are you okay?"

"Ja." He licked his lips. "My apologies, kids. I got lost in thought." And eavesdropping. *Lord, forgive me.* He clapped his hands. "Okay, now we're going to learn about Joseph from the Old Testament. How many of you have heard of him?"

Several hands shot up.

"Good. Shout out things you know about Joseph."

"He had lots of brothers—"

"He was a slave—"

"He went to Egypt—"

"His mama's name was Rachel—"

"His papa was Jacob—"

Smiling, Olav nodded. "Goodness, aren't you all smart? His life is interesting, isn't it? Growing up in a large family with all those boys and only one girl. But his brothers didn't like him because they thought he was their parents' favorite, and perhaps he was. So, they got mad and wanted to kill him, but his oldest brother said no. Instead, they threw him in a well, and then later sold him to some merchants."

"That wasn't very nice," Roy said.

"No, it wasn't." His gaze swept the group. "But we aren't always nice, are we? Think about times you did mean things to your brothers or sisters or friends. We get upset or angry at others and lash out, often saying or doing things that are unkind."

"What happened to him?" Astrid piped up. "Did he ever see his family again?"

"God used his situation for good. Joseph proved himself to be trustworthy, and the king, who is called a pharaoh, promoted him." He winked at Astrid. "And, yes, he saw his family again. There was a famine where they lived. A famine is when the crops don't grow, so the people don't have food to eat. His brothers went to Egypt to ask for help, and they didn't recognize him. Joseph had one of his employees put a cup into one of his brother's bags, to make it seem like they were stealing."

"Why would he do that?"

"He wanted to test them. Maybe he wanted to see if they would they give up their brother as easily as they had given up him. There are many reasons why people do things, sometimes for good and sometimes to cause trouble. Was Joseph's reason good or bad?"

"Good—"

"Bad—"

"Bad—"

"Good—"

Olav chuckled. "The Bible can be confusing, can't it? We have to dig deep to see what God is telling us." His mouth dropped open. Was God using his story time with the kids to teach him a lesson, too? He'd decided to talk about Joseph weeks ago, long before Hazel arrived, but had God inspired him to choose this particular Bible character knowing he'd be struggling to accept her claims of innocence, clinging to a niggling doubt that she might have stolen the items, even if justifiably?

Did she feel his hesitation? No, not hesitation. Mistrust. He had to be honest with himself. He didn't believe her story, and he was unconvinced she'd been sent by God. Was she like Joseph's brother, Benjamin, framed for a crime she didn't commit? How could he determine the truth?

A Family for Hazel

Chapter Ten

An hour later, Hazel wandered toward the church to retrieve her supplies for the next activity. Her conversation with Dagmar had gone well, and the little girl's mood had lightened. She promised to talk with her dad in the near future about how she felt, but she wasn't sure when. She'd asked to remain with Hazel the rest of the day as her helper, and Olav had agreed, looking at the two of them with admiration and another emotion she couldn't fathom. He continued to be an enigma, but perhaps she'd understand him more as time passed.

She waved at Dagmar, who she'd left entertaining the youngsters. Supervised by Mrs. Gjerstad, and her face wreathed in smiles, Olav's daughter led them in a game of *Bro Bro Brille*, a Norwegian version of the London Bridge game she'd grown up playing. Convinced the two had the kids fully occupied, Hazel ducked inside the cool, dim recesses of the church and breathed a sigh of relief. Alone, at last.

Skirts swishing, she made her way down the corridor to the small room where she and Olav had stashed the materials for the week. Anxious at first, she'd come into her own with the four- and five-year-old kids. Wide-eyed, they listened to her tell the Bible stories and had thrown themselves into the crafts with wonder and excitement. She was making a difference, more so than she'd ever done in her life. And that wouldn't have happened if it weren't for James Agnew's nefarious actions to frame her. Perhaps God had used the bad in her life for a purpose. She'd have to think on that later.

Did the other servants believe his lies? The maid who had been there when James *found* the jewels had stood by her, but would she attest to Hazel's innocence to the rest of the staff? Her friend, Betsy, had housed her, declaring James's actions deplorable, but would she go out of her way to defend Hazel's honor? The Agnews were powerful and well regarded in Waynesboro. Who would believe the word of a servant or woman of little means? Her lips twisted. No one.

"Stop." She rummaged through the boxes to find her materials. "You have a new life now. There's no reason to dwell on the past."

Quiet laughter sounded from somewhere in the building, followed by muffled voices. Had someone followed her inside, or were they already here? She crept into the hallway and cocked her head.

"Wait until I show you what my sister sent in the mail." Paper crinkled, then, "That Hazel woman has a sullied past. I wonder if our pastor knows about it. Look at this clipping. It mentions a woman named Hazel Markham. That must be our pastor's bride-to-be."

Hazel gasped, then clamped a hand over her mouth, trembling. She froze. Had they heard her?

"Are you sure it's her?"

"It's got to be. How many Hazels are there, and she's from Pennsylvania."

"Humph. You can't trust those mail-order brides. You know Vanessa Anderson was one, and I've heard things about her."

"Really?" The word dripped with curiosity. "Do tell."

"Read the newspaper article first. Hazel is a thief. She worked for a very important family in Pennsylvania, and she had the audacity to steal from them. I find it interesting that they didn't press charges. Someone like that should be in jail."

Tears sprang to Hazel's eyes. So much for keeping the story out of the newspaper. James claimed he didn't want the incident to be public, but had he leaked the information as another way to punish her? What were the odds that someone here would have relatives in Waynesboro?

"I agree," one of the women scoffed. "We can't have a thief as our pastor's wife. We should tell him about this."

"I heard he found her through an agency. You would think they would look into her background before farming her out to some unsuspecting man."

"Maybe she paid the agency to make the information go away."

A gasp. "You think?"

"It's a possibility. Have you finished the article? Read the letter. My sister says in addition to stealing, she heard Hazel threw herself at the son. What made her think the man would marry the likes of her, a servant? She's obviously money hungry."

Balling her hands into fists, Hazel pressed her lips together. Should she march down the hall and confront the women? Tell them the article was false, and that the letter was full of lies and innuendo. Would it do any good? A chill swept over her. The encounter might prompt them to drag her in front of the entire church. They might do that anyway.

"And she has managed to pull the wool over the congregation's eyes. Do you see how the other ladies fawn over her? What fools. They're going to wake up and find that she's stolen from them, too."

"You're right. She got caught in Pennsylvania, so she came out here for fresh pickings."

Hazel cringed. Would she ever be free of her past? Hundreds of miles from James, and he was still ruining her life.

"I've heard just about enough, you two," Olav's voice reverberated. "I've a mind to bring you before the elders for your gossiping and backbiting, but we will handle this among ourselves for now."

"You misunderstood us."

"No, I haven't. I heard almost the entire conversation. The venom in your voices was quite clear, as were your judgmental attitudes. I am well aware of the situation, and no matter what your letter claims, the allegations against Miss Markham are false."

"But—"

"I'm not finished." His tone was like sharpened steel. "What you are obviously unaware of is that Miss Markham is here in the church, and may have heard every one of your hurtful words. I expect better from my congregation. We are to love others and to build them up. Ephesians says, 'Let no corrupt communication proceed out of your mouth, but that which is good to the use of edifying, that it may minister in grace unto the hearers.' And Titus tells us to speak evil of no one. And there are plenty of admonishments in Proverbs about what you've done here."

Hazel wrapped her arms around her middle. Tears tumbled down her cheeks as pain and embarrassment mingled with gratitude and relief. Olav had come to her rescue. Her husband-to-be had taken the women to task for their words. Would they regret their actions, or would his reprimand only make them hate her more?

A Family for Hazel

Chapter Eleven

The murmur of conversation mingled with the clinking of silverware on china as Hazel nibbled at her food. Olav had made arrangements for Dagmar to stay with the Andersens for the evening, then invited Hazel to dinner at one of the nicer restaurants in town. Unused to eating in such a fine establishment, she peeked at the other diners for guidance. There was more silverware flanking her plate than she used in a week.

Seated in the back, they had privacy from prying eyes. The day had finished well, but the hurt from the two busybodies still stung. After he'd finished rebuking them, Olav sent them from the church, then came looking for her. She admitted she heard the entire conversation but had no time to discuss the incident because the children were waiting for her. That's when he'd invited her to dinner.

She figured he'd take her to one of the rustic places in town for a quick meal and discussion, but they'd been at the restaurant for an hour thus far, and he had yet to bring up the topic. Instead, he'd regaled her with stories about his growing-up years and early days as a pastor, sharing foibles and mistakes that gently poked fun at his naïveté.

Crinkled at the corners, his green eyes sparkled in the candlelight that glistened against his ash-blond hair curled against his collar. A stubborn lock fell over his forehead no matter how many times he brushed it away. What would it feel like to run her fingers through the silky-looking strands?

Olav pushed away his empty plate, then wiped his mouth. "You're doing a wonderful job with the children. The Pied Piper has nothing on you."

Warmth filled her, and she ducked her head. "Thank you. I didn't expect to enjoy it as much as I do, but their curiosity and openness is a joy to work with. They have so many questions! Fortunately, I've been able to answer them, but I'm waiting for the day one of them blurts out something outside my knowledge base."

"It's okay to tell them you don't know." He smiled at her over his coffee cup. "We can search for the answer together. I'd like that."

"Me, too." She rubbed at a spot on the tablecloth. "But I'll stick to flannel boards and drawing for now."

He chuckled. "You should hear some of the questions that are posed to me. It's exciting to have congregants digging in the scriptures, but I'm terrified of leading them astray if I mess up an interpretation."

She cocked her head. "You seem so self-assured."

"Hardly."

"Well, I have already learned much from you, and I'm sure the people of the church can say the same." She cleared her throat. "Thank you for coming to my rescue. I was conflicted about what to do. If I'm honest, my earthly-self wanted to slap them, but that wouldn't have helped." She rubbed her chest. "But it also aches. I thought the pain would have gone away by now, but their words keep popping into my mind. How can they be so mean when they barely know me?"

He took her fingers in his and stroked the back of her hand with his thumb.

Hazel shivered at his touch.

With a grin, he winked. "Don't be shocked, but if they'd have been men, I might have given in to the desire to do that very thing." He sobered. "But you're right. Violence is never an answer between individuals. I'd like for all of us to meet so they can apologize for their behavior, and I'm still unsure whether or not to bring them to the elders."

She broke out into a cold sweat. "Do we have to meet? Can't you just let the admonishment stand? I will do my best to treat them with kindness and respect."

"Ah, 'to heap burning coals on their heads.'"

"Something like that."

A frown twisted his lips. "I must be doing something wrong if the church has people like these two ladies. I've failed in my teachings."

"No." She put her other hand on top of his. "People are going to do what they will. You can lead them, but ultimately it is their decision as to how they act and respond to the message of God." A sigh slipped out. "And hopefully, these are the only two who are like this." She licked her lips. Oh, if only that were true, but her experience with women told her differently. No matter what their income or class, there was a certain number of ladies who enjoyed gossip and talking about people behind their backs. In fact, some seemed to thrive on the drama and intrigue, making up what they didn't know. "Perhaps a sermon would do the trick."

"Brilliant." He gave her a saucy smile. "And you can help me write it."

She giggled. "Oh, no. I'll leave that to you. I work best with the children."

"But some of the adults act like children."

"True, but you're on your own."

Squeezing her fingers, he cleared his throat. "Listen, I would be willing to leave the church and find another if you're uncomfortable here. Perhaps a move would put your past behind you."

Her pulse raced. "You would change churches for me?"

"Ja."

"That means a lot, but this one incident isn't a reason to leave. Let's see where God leads you."

"Us. Leads us. Don't forget we're partners."

She sagged against the chair as tension seeped from her shoulders. How many men would give up a good position for their wives? Few that she knew. How blessed she was that God had provided this man.

Setting his coffee cup on the table, Olav laced his fingers in his lap. He'd blurted out the proposal to find another church without thinking, then regretted the impulse. To his relief, she turned him down. He wanted to make her happy, put the sparkle in her eyes that he'd seen in response to his offer, but if he wasn't careful, his knee-jerk reactions would get him into trouble.

A sermon was definitely in order. Hazel seemed to want to believe the two women were the only gossips in the church. Unfortunately, he knew differently. This incident wasn't the first time members of the congregation were guilty of idle talk and speculation. The newspaper article had obviously been accepted as gospel by the ladies, giving fuel to their fire.

He was just as bad with his doubts about his bride-to-be, and his reprimand to the women had been pointed at himself as much as to them. He needed to shed his apprehension about Hazel once and for all. Why couldn't he trust that Miss Milton had performed her due diligence? Should he do his own background check? He needed to consider how the situation would affect Dagmar, and his ministry. If the story leaked to people outside the church, would they judge him as a hypocrite by preaching purity yet marrying a thief?

Trust Me.

A shiver raced up Olav's back. He rarely heard God's audible voice, his heavenly Father normally choosing to speak to him through the

Scriptures or fellow believers. He wanted to trust. He wanted to believe in her innocence, but uncertainty continued to plague him.

Trust Me.

"Are you all right, Olav?" Concern wrinkled Hazel's forehead.

"What? Yes." He rolled his eyes. "Sorry. How rude of me. I got lost in thought."

"There is much to think about with this situation. You have every right to be worried about how it will impact the church, and more importantly, Dagmar."

His eyes widened. "Ja. Thank you for understanding. She is everything to me."

"Of course. We must protect her." Hazel propped her elbows on the table and steepled her fingers. "I will go along with whatever you decide. I've not been here long, and I would like to see our agreement through to marry, but should you determine that my...uh...history...would damage her in any way, we will contact Miss Milton to make other arrangements for me."

He shook his head. He would not let the malicious behaviors separate him from this woman. He didn't know how, but he'd come to care about Hazel. Not love. It was too soon for that, but her sweet spirit was working its way into his heart. And the incident in the church had generated a fierce desire to protect her, make her feel safe and free from blame.

He wanted her to be innocent, so she could stay and be his wife, and a mother to Dagmar. He'd been alone for a long time. He'd agreed to the marriage to keep his job, then after he made the arrangements he realized that having a wife would provide Dagmar with a mama, something the child deserved. But in a matter of days, he'd come to look forward to his upcoming nuptials. There was a huge "I told you so" coming from Miles, which he would gladly accept.

"Not going to happen." Olav got up and squatted next to her. He grasped her shoulders. "Believe me when I say that we will get through this. The evildoers will not succeed. God is with us, and He will pave the way to work this out for our good. He will receive the glory when all is said and done. And I will be proud to be your husband." He stroked her jaw, astonished that he'd meant every word.

Chapter Twelve

Applause filled the sanctuary, and the children giggled and bowed as the sound of their singing faded. Hazel beamed and caught Olav's eye where he stood behind the pulpit. He raised his hands to quell the noise. "Weren't they wonderful? We had a blessed week, with many of your sons and daughters professing their love for Jesus. We hope you will join us for cake and punch outside." He stepped down, and one of the elders stopped him, his face set in a scowl.

Now what? Her heart thudded in her chest. Must they speak to him every time he darkened the doorway of the church? Two of them had collared him after last week's sermon, and one of them had come by midweek during camp. With a deep sigh, she turned toward the door. She'd better get used to their presence and their interference.

She made her way outside and squinted against the glare. Heat from the sun's rays warmed her scalp, and she pulled up her bonnet. Several of the women were busy setting up the refreshments, and she hurried to the table. "What may I do to help?"

Mrs. Davies, an elderly woman in her eighties, looked up from slicing the cake. "Would you be a dear and serve the punch?"

"Certainly."

"I'll give you a hand." A woman came around the corner carrying a box of drinking vessels and set the carton on the ground. "I found a stash in one of the Sunday school rooms. I'm Mrs. Lange, in case you can't remember."

Hazel nodded, then ladled the sweet concoction into the cups as fast as Mrs. Lange put them on the table. The woman hummed softly as she worked, then tucked away the empty box. "I'd say we work together quite nicely, Miss Markham."

"Thank you. I'm still trying to get my feet under me."

"Well, it's hard to tell." The woman patted her shoulder. "You are a natural with the children. You have a real calling. Were you a teacher in Pennsylvania?"

"No. I...uh...was a lady's maid." Had Mrs. Lange not heard the gossip or been privy to the newspaper article? "There were no little ones in the household." Why had she said that?

"A shame." Mrs. gestured to a group of kids. "But you'll have plenty of opportunity before you and the pastor start your family."

Before Hazel could think of a reply, members of the congregation crowded the table to avail themselves of the food. For the next twenty minutes, she filled cups, handed out napkins, and conversed with the men and women. Her cheeks ached from smiling, but her heart was full. Everyone had complimented her on the program and protested when she tried to explain her part in the planning had been minimal. They were gracious and welcoming, and she received copious invitations for tea.

No one seemed to study her with suspicion. Their questions seemed born of curiosity and interest rather than probing. Had the two awful women seen the error of their ways and refrained from spreading their rumors and lies? Was the sermon Olav planned for tomorrow necessary? She glanced around the yard but didn't see the pair among the celebrants.

The crowd around the food tables dissipated, and Mrs. Davies waved her away. "Go chat with some of the ladies. You've worked enough."

"You'll be okay on your own?"

The elderly woman chortled and motioned to a chair. "I'll park myself right there and be just fine. Go be with others your own age. No need to stay with this old gal."

Hazel smiled. "You're not old."

"Oh, honey, aren't you sweet? I'll be ninety-two in three months if the good Lord doesn't take me home before then."

"Goodness. I never would have guessed."

"You wouldn't be blowin' wind up an old lady's skirts, would you?"

Her cheeks warmed, and Hazel sputtered, "Of course not."

"I'm teasin' you." Mrs. Davies grinned and waddled to the chair. "You know you gotta be a sight less gullible if you're going to succeed as a pastor's wife. No tellin' what people will say or do. Now, get on with you."

After a last glance at the elderly woman, Hazel made her way across the churchyard. Where was Olav? She'd caught sight of him several times while serving, but he seemed to have disappeared. Had the elders commandeered his time yet again? She frowned. Should she dream up a reason to interrupt them? Would he be irritated or grateful?

Neck swiveling, she continued to search for his ash-blond head and broad-shouldered frame among the sea of people. Where was he?

"Good job, Miss Markham."

"Enjoyed the kids' program, Miss Markham."

She lifted her hand in acknowledgment as folks called out to her. If she wasn't careful, all the praise would go to her head. Perhaps she should look inside the church for Olav. As she approached the building, voices floated toward her. She look behind herself, then craned her neck to check behind a copse of nearby trees. Nothing. She got closer, then peeked around the corner.

About halfway down the side of the building, Olav and the sheriff stood with their backs to her. Hands shoved into his pockets, Sheriff Baas rocked on his heels. "I'm not sure how long it will take to get the information, Olav. These things take time."

"I know, and I'm not in too much of a hurry, but I would like to know before the wedding."

Tears sprang to Hazel's eyes. Olav still thought she was guilty. She pulled back so they wouldn't see her and pressed herself against the clapboard siding.

"Not a problem. The Pinkertons are the best in the business and will ferret out the truth. Don't you worry about that."

"I appreciate your help, Erik." Olav huffed a sigh and finger-combed his hair. "You're a good friend."

"You'd do the same for me."

Footsteps sounded, and Hazel picked up her skirts and bolted through the thinning crowd. He claimed he believed her. Were his words a lie, or had something changed his mind? Her chin trembled as she fled, her mind racing. What were her options? She couldn't marry a man who mistrusted her, but she couldn't leave without so much as a by-your-leave. Would Miss Milton find her another groom if Olav rejected her? Had he already contacted the agency? Was she doomed to a life of running from her problems?

A Family for Hazel

Chapter Thirteen

The wagon creaked as it lumbered down the pitted dirt road, muddied from yesterday's rain. Olav held the reins loosely in his hands, the mare barely needed his leading to find her way to Miles' and Vanessa's place. He snuck a peek at Hazel from under the brim of his hat. She sat ramrod straight next to him, looking neither left nor right, and her hands clasped in her lap. Her chin jutted forward, and her lips were pursed. What thoughts created such an expression?

She'd left the Bible camp celebration early yesterday, then refused to see him when he'd called on her, claiming a headache. She made her own way to church this morning and given him monosyllabic answers to his questions. Dark half-moon smudges below her eyes attested to her lack of sleep, but he sensed there was more to her silence than feeling unwell. She'd sat through the service staring at a spot behind him, then moved mechanically when it was time to go.

Taken from the third chapter of James, his sermon about the harm and good that could be done by the tongue seemed to have affected more than the two abashed-looking women in the back pew. Several members of the congregation had reddened or ducked their heads as he preached.

Had they been speculating about his wife, or were there other issues at play? Next week he would share stories about Barnabas and his abilities to encourage fellow believers, but it seemed his bride-to-be could use comfort before then. Was she angry at him, or had something happened at the festivities?

Dagmar sat between Hazel and him, whispering to her ever-present rag doll. The cloth figure had seen better days, but it was the last one Sigrid had made for his daughter, so he was loathe to throw it away. How did Hazel feel about seeing the remnants of his late wife's presence in their lives?

A hot, stiff breeze tugged at his hat, and he glanced at the sky to see if they were in for a storm, then pulled the Stetson lower on his forehead. Fluffy, white clouds were scattered high in the blue expanse, so it appeared the beautiful day might be theirs for the near future. However, he'd learned early that the weather could change in an instant here in the Midwest.

They arrived at the Andersens', and he pulled on the reins. "Whoa." The wagon lumbered to a stop, and Olav jumped to the ground, then turned to lift Dagmar out of the conveyance. Hazel climbed down on the other side, further evidence that she seemed out of sorts with him. He huffed out a sigh. Hopefully, time with Andersens would solve whatever was bothering her.

A shriek sounded, and Vanessa flew off the porch to envelope Hazel, who looked shocked at the effusive display of affection. Dagmar giggled and threw herself at Miles. His best friend swept her into his arms and gave her a resounding kiss on the cheek. "And how are you, little one?"

"Hungry."

Miles threw his head back and laughed, and Olav smiled. "I think he wanted to know how you're feeling, Daughter."

She cocked her head, her eyebrows scrunched together in confusion. "I'm feeling hungry."

He shook his head, a smile still tugging at his lips. "Then we better hope Mrs. Andersen is ready for you, ja?"

With one arm looped around Hazel's waist, Vanessa gestured toward the house with the other. "Dinner is served, and there is plenty for us, Miss Dagmar."

"Yay!" Dagmar clapped her hands, and Miles set her down. She galloped up the steps and raced into the house, her white-blonde braids bouncing.

Olav rolled his eyes at Vanessa. "My apologies for Dagmar. I'm still working on her manners."

"Nonsense." Vanessa tucked a loose strand behind her ear. "She's a delightful child and well behaved. She shouldn't have to stand on formalities with us." She grinned and rubbed her stomach. "Besides, I'm ready to eat, too."

They trooped into the house, and worked together to move the food from the stove to the table and pour water into the cups. After they were seated, Miles blessed the food, then they filled their plates with the fragrant delicacies.

Dagmar stabbed a meatball. "Yum! Kjøttkaker, my favorite."

"You say that about everything." Vanessa scooped mushy peas onto her fork.

"Because you are a good cook."

Miles snickered and nudged his wife. "That wasn't always the case. Well, she could make American dishes, but we had to teach her how to make Norwegian food."

Hazel nibbled a small bite of the succulent meatball, then wiped her mouth. "Did it take you a long time to get acclimated? I feel like a fish out of water."

"You've not even been here a month. Getting comfortable won't happen overnight." Vanessa smirked. "I'm not sure what was more difficult, learning to keep house or live with this guy. Coming here was a huge change."

"Why did you come?" Hazel took a sip of water. "Did you have no other choice."

A shadow crossed Vanessa's face, then she smiled. "I could have stayed where I was, but I needed a fresh start. You see, I found my fiancé in the arms of another woman a short time before we were to be married. I called off the wedding, of course, but I got tired of the sidelong glances and conversations that ceased when I entered a room. I hadn't done anything wrong, but some had the opinion his...straying was somehow my fault."

"How terrible." Hazel's eyes widened.

Vanessa shrugged. "Frederick and I didn't love each other, but it hurt to be subjected to his infidelity. My parents wanted the match to secure his wealth. Anyway, he is a distant memory, and finding Miles was the best thing that ever happened."

"Didn't you find it hard to trust him after...you know."

"Absolutely. We had a rocky start, didn't we, honey."

Miles nodded and slipped his arm around her shoulders. "For good or bad, our past shapes us. We can be victimized by the bad, or we can rise above it."

Hazel stiffened, and she glanced at Olav. "Easier said than done, don't you think? Especially when the past refuses to go away."

He swallowed a sigh. What was she trying to say? He'd addressed the gossiping, and no one else in the church seemed to know or care about her employer's claim of thievery. Would he ever understand this woman enough to have a real relationship? Did she want one, or did she regret her decision to come to Wisconsin?

A Family for Hazel

Chapter Fourteen

Swollen black clouds hovered overhead, and a cold breeze swirled around the wagon. Hazel pulled her thin shawl closer, praying the storm would hold off until they got her back to the boarding house. She glanced at Olav who gripped the reins in tight hands, the golden blond hairs on his arms stark against his tanned skin. Eyes riveted on the road ahead, his mouth was set in a slash as he guided the skittish horse toward their destination.

She frowned as the bitter taste of regret filled her mouth. She should have accepted the invitation to spend the night, but all she wanted to do was be alone. Exhausted from putting on a smile and pretending that every reference to the saintly Sigrid didn't cut her like a knife, she wanted to curl up on the bed with her head under the covers. Maybe a drenching rain would wash away the disappointment at the realization Olav was never going to get over his first wife.

The wagon lurched into a large hole, and she was thrown against him. Her hand landed on his thigh, tight with thick muscles. A tingle shot from her palm to her shoulder, and she yanked away as if burned. "Sorry," she squeaked. Heat suffused her face. Sitting in the back with Dagmar would be safer. She wouldn't risk getting thrown from the vehicle or losing her heart to the handsome Norwegian sitting next to her.

Why did she think she could marry a widower? According to Miss Milton, Olav's wife had been gone for over five years. Why wasn't the woman a distant memory by this time? Guilt pricked Hazel. Losing her parents wasn't the same thing as the death of a spouse, but she continued to feel their absence. Of course he would still miss his wife. She'd been a fool to think otherwise.

What was the adage? Something about playing second fiddle. That's what she would be. He would spend the rest of their lives comparing her to Sigrid. Did he see his wife every time he looked at Dagmar. With her silky, white-blonde hair and crystal-blue eyes, how much did the little girl resemble her mother? Hazel swallowed a sigh. Her mousy brown hair and nondescript brown eyes must be a letdown for Olav.

"Are we almost home, Papa? I'm cold."

He tossed a glance behind him. "Almost, honey. Pull the quilt up over your head to block the wind."

"I'll sit with her."

"No, I want to be up front with you." Dagmar stood up and grabbed Hazel's shoulder. "I'm missing all the fun."

Olav chuckled and brought the wagon to a stop. "Hardly, Daughter, but come on up."

Dragging the quilt with her, she clambered over the board and squeezed between Hazel and Olav to plop onto the front seat. She wriggled and wrestled with the patchwork cover until she'd tucked it around herself and Hazel. "Okay, Papa, you can drive now."

His left eyebrow raised, and his lips quirked. "Well, thank you very much." He slapped the horse's rump with the traces, and the wagon jerked forward.

"See, isn't this better?" Face inches away, Dagmar nestled close and grinned at Hazel. "We're warmer together."

"Yes." Hazel returned her smile and studied the child's smooth, glowing complexion whose features seemed to be carved from marble. Golden flecks gave her blue eyes a greenish cast. Had she inherited that from her father? "You're a smart little girl." Beautiful, intelligent, and sweet, probably just like her mother.

She poked Dagmar. "Tell me a story. Can I assume you have a favorite Norwegian fairy tale?" Anything to get her mind off the constant reminder of the former Mrs. Kristensen.

"Okay." With a wide grin, the little girl straightened and cleared her throat. "Once upon a time there was a man who was cranky and cross. He didn't think his wife did anything right in the house. So, one night during haymaking time, he came home and scolded her. His wife was used to him and said, 'Don't be angry. Tomorrow let's change places. You can mind the house, and I'll mow.' He thought that was perfect, so the next morning his wife took the scythe and went to the hayfield."

"She must have been a strong woman," Hazel said. "I couldn't do that."

Olav winked. "Good thing you're marrying a preacher."

"You're interrupting, Papa."

"Sorry, go on, little one."

"So the man wanted to churn the butter, but then he got thirsty and went to the cellar for some ale. When he was down there, he heard the pig come into the kitchen overhead and knock over the churn. The man raced upstairs, and the pig was licking up the cream he'd spilled. The farmer shooed the pig outside and went to the dairy to get more cream. Back in the house, he began to churn, but then remembered the cow needed to be fed and milked. But the field was too far, so he decided to put her on the house that was thatched with sod."

"The roof," Hazel exclaimed. "How in the world would he get the cow on the roof?"

"You have to wait and see, Miss Hazel." Dagmar's eyes twinkled. "First, he needed to feed and water her. But he suddenly remembered his son was in the house and probably crawling around, so he went back inside to get the churn. He didn't want the little boy to knock over the churn like the pig had done."

"He forgot about his child?" Hazel pressed a hand against her bodice. "What kind of man is this?"

"You remember this is a fairy tale, right?" Olav chuckled.

"And obviously not based on any sort of reality." She returned his smile. "Go on, Dagmar."

"He strapped the churn to his back, then grabbed the bucket to get some water. But when he leaned over the well, the cream ran out of the churn, all over his back and down into the well. He untied the churn and tossed it on the ground, then filled the bucket and watered the cow. By now, it was nearly lunchtime, and he hadn't made the butter yet, but he thought he should boil some porridge, the only thing he knew how to make. He put a pot of water on the fire to boil, then went back outside to take the cow onto the roof. The house was built close into the hill, so he put a board down and walked the cow across it."

"How clever." Hazel clapped her hands.

"I told you it would work out." Dagmar sent her a self-satisfied smile.

"Yes, you did."

"We're coming to the best part." She crossed her arms. "He was afraid the cow might fall off the roof and get hurt, so he tied a rope around her, then slipped the rope down the chimney and went into the kitchen where he tied it to his leg. By now the water had boiled, but he hadn't ground the oats, so he started to grind. And grind. And grind. But then the cow fell off the roof and dragged the man up the chimney by the rope. He was stuck fast, and the cow hung halfway down the wall." Dagmar giggled. "Anyway, his wife was getting hungry, and she went home. When she got there she found such a sight, the cow swinging and bawling, so she rushed forward and used her scythe to cut the rope. From inside there came a loud clatter because her husband had fallen out of the chimney. She ran into the kitchen and found him standing on his head in the porridge pot."

Hazel laughed and gave Dagmar a quick one-armed hug. "What a wonderful story, and you told it very well." She cast a sidelong glance at Olav. "And I'll bet you enjoyed it because the tale proves men should never do housework."

He snickered and shook his head. "I've done my fair share. No, but it was Sigrid's favorite. She told it to Dagmar often at bedtime."

Nibbling on the inside of her cheek, Hazel sagged in the seat. She'd escaped her predecessor for a short time, but the woman's presence had returned to the wagon, proving that Olav would never forget her, never love Hazel as he'd loved her. Was the chance to be Dagmar's mother enough of a reason to stay and marry her father?

Chapter Fifteen

Back aching, Hazel yanked the last weed from the garden in front of Olav's house and tossed it onto the pile. She straightened and stretched her arms over her head. Her spine popped and crackled. Brushing an errant strand of hair out of her eyes, she surveyed the flower bed and smiled.

Over the course of the week since their visit with Miles and Vanessa, Olav had been gracious and giving. Only once had he mentioned Sigrid, and the comment had been made in passing. What had happened to create the change? Had he realized how the constant references to his late wife made her feel?

One night while wrestling with sleep, memories of Mother invaded her thoughts: curled up together on the divan reading, sitting on the wraparound porch sipping lemonade, sauntering across the lawn talking about everything and nothing. Tears sprang to Hazel's eyes as a light breeze stroked her cheeks. She wouldn't be in Wisconsin if her mother hadn't died, but she could use her wisdom and guidance.

Snippets of conversations floated through her mind, and she sighed. Mother would tell her she was being impatient as usual. Expecting Olav and her to be in perfect sync after a month. She climbed to her feet and glanced at her groom-to-be, who was painting the front door of the house. His muscles strained against his shirt as he moved the brush up and down on the wood. Gracious, but he was a handsome man.

Her stomach buzzed as if she'd swallowed a hummingbird, and she pressed one hand against her middle. She should apologize for her behavior before he regretted bringing her to Green Bay...if he didn't already rue the decision. She walked up the steps. "Listen, Olav...I...uh—"

"Ja?" Brush in hand, he turned, his green eyes piercing her face. "You need help with the garden? I'm almost finished here."

"No. The garden is done." She gestured to the boxes he'd hung on the railing. "I'm going to fill the planters next. That's not why I interrupted."

He set the brush on top of the can. "Is everything okay?"

"No...yes...well, I just want to say I'm sorry...for how I've been acting. I've been, uh, difficult and standoffish."

A smile lit his face. "There is no need to apologize. We are both struggling to find our way down this path. I appreciate your patience with me. You deserve the same." His smile faltered. "And perhaps I've not been as welcoming as I should be."

Her breath whooshed out, and the knots in her shoulders unkinked. "No, no. You've been fine." Her fingers plucked at her skirts. "Anyway, that's all. I should get back to work."

"Thank you for reaching out. I'm not good at talking about feelings, but I have learned communication is important. I will try to get better." He grabbed a rag from beside the paint can and wiped his hands. "And now I will help you put the flowers in the boxes."

"I can do—"

"Nonsense. The door is done, and my other chores can wait."

"Okay." She gestured to the collection of plants Vanessa had brought for her at church yesterday. "I'm not sure what these are, but Vanessa said they would be happy in the sun."

He nodded. "She is gifted in her knowledge of flowers." He trotted down the stairs, picked up one of the crates filled with flowers and carried it onto the porch. He returned for the second crate while she put a shovelful of dirt in each planter.

She bent to retrieve one of the plants, and her fingers grazed Olav's, who had reached in the box. She jumped, a tremor shooting up her arm. "I didn't see you."

With a chuckle, he held out the flower. "I will hand them to you, so you don't have to keep bending."

"Thank you." Her face warm, she accepted the leafy stem filled with buds. Why did she have to blush at the slightest provocation? He must think her a ninny. She tucked the root ball into the box and reached for the next plant. Their fingers touched again, and she shivered. Stop!

They worked in tandem for several minutes until all the flowers were nestled into the planters. She poured water over them, then descended the stairs. He jogged down the steps and winked, then held out his hand. "Job well done, *Miss Markham*. Vanessa would be proud."

Giggling, she shook his proffered hand. "You, too, *Mr. Kristensen.*"

He grinned, then pulled his handkerchief from his pocket and rubbed her forehead. "Hold still. You've got a smudge."

She froze, but her heart thudded in her chest. Why did her body betray her? She knew she didn't dare care for him. Not with his late wife in the forefront of his mind.

A wagon rattled behind them, and they turned. Two of the elders, Mr. Calland and Mr. Rendahl, if she remembered correctly, sat bolt upright in a buckboard, their drawn eyebrows and dark frowns mirror images of each other. Olav stiffened beside her and stuffed the hanky into his pocket, then lifted his hand in greeting. He was apparently not happy to see them either.

The conveyance rolled to a stop, the leather harness squeaking as Mr. Calland tied off the reins, then climbed to the ground, followed by Mr. Rendahl.

"Gentleman." Olav nodded. "What can I do for you today?"

Looking down his nose, Mr. Calland said, "We've come to inform you that we have made arrangements for you to marry immediately."

"What?" Olav's eyes narrowed.

Hazel gasped, then clamped her lips together. What happened to waiting until the end of next month?

"And it appears the decision has been made none too soon."

"Excuse me?" Fists clenched, Olav leaned toward the man. "What do you mean by that comment?"

"The elders have met and have determined that the time you spend together at the house alone is inappropriate. You must lead by example, and the example you're setting is unacceptable."

Nausea swept over Hazel, and she swallowed lest she lose her breakfast.

"First of all, Finn, we are not alone. Dagmar is here at all times. Secondly, you have just insulted Miss Markham, which is *unacceptable.*"

The man had the grace to flush, but he continued to glare at Olav. "She came to marry you. There is no reason to wait. We have made arrangements with a circuit preacher, and he will arrive in two weeks. Be ready to wed."

Olav crossed his arms. "Only if Miss Markham agrees. I will not have her forced into the wedding. I don't appreciate your innuendos. Our behavior has been above reproach."

"But—"

"No buts. I respect you, and I thought you held me in esteem. However, that doesn't seem to be the case. Furthermore, I agreed to your terms of marrying by the end of next month. If Hazel is willing to do so earlier, then we will wed when the preacher comes. Otherwise, you will wait along with the rest of the congregation. Is that clear?"

The man's gaze slid to Hazel. She stuffed her dirt-encrusted hands into the pockets of her work-worn dress and gulped. Olav had defended her honor. She owed it to him to agree to marry in two weeks. Would she be ready?

Chapter Sixteen

Hands on his hips, Olav watched the wagon disappear around the bend in the road. He pushed his hat back on his head and huffed out a breath. He'd meant what he said. He respected the men, but he was tired of them interfering with his life. Was it too much to expect some semblance of privacy, or was he being stubborn and arrogant?

It's okay. Really." Hazel laid her hand on his arm. "They *are* correct. I came here to marry you, so why not get it over and done." Her cheeks pinked. "Wait, that came out wrong."

He quirked one eyebrow and grinned. "I know." He sobered. "I just don't appreciate their attitudes of assuming the worst about us...you."

She shrugged. "As you may recall, this isn't the first time people have believed untrue things about me. I guess I'm used to it. I don't like it, but I guess I have to accept that it's going to happen."

"I'm not convinced the congregation has concerns. I think this comes from them."

Perhaps, but as the Bible says, 'Let no man put a stumbling block or an occasion to fall in his brother's way.' We know nothing is going on, but if the elders have doubts, we must do what is best for them."

"Wise words. Now, who's the preacher?" He shot her a saucy smile, but his pulse skipped. He'd let his pride get in the way, because he'd been embarrassed by the elders' visit. *Lord, forgive me, and thank You for sending Hazel.*

A smile bloomed on her face, and she waved her hand in a dismissive gesture. "I'll settle for being the preacher's wife. It's a beautiful day, and they can't take that away from us. I still have to weed the vegetable garden. Do you want to help, or do you have other chores?"

"I'll get Dagmar. We'll both help." He tugged his Stetson low on his forehead and trotted toward the dirt yard where his daughter skipped rope.

How could he have thought Hazel plain? True, she didn't have Sigrid's Nordic looks, but her brown hair was shot with red and gold highlights, giving it the color of cinnamon, and her chocolate-colored eyes snapped with intelligence. Her complexion was smooth like Sigrid's, although not as fair. Rather than narrow like his late wife's face, Hazel's was heart shaped with a pointed chin. Her shapely curves filled her dresses in all the right places, totally unlike Sigrid's slender form.

He froze. Was he finally ready to make room in his heart for another woman? Miles had said Sigrid would want him to be happy, but he'd never really believed the statement. Guilt over her death had filled him for so long, he didn't know how to live without the regret. If she hadn't come to Wisconsin, his wife would still be alive, wouldn't she?

She'd always had a delicate constitution, and the harsh winters had been difficult for her, then she'd never fully recovered from Dagmar's birth.

I call home whom I will.

Olav's knees buckled, but he caught himself and managed to stay on his feet. The words resounded in his head...and his soul. How could he preach about God's will and God's plans for people's lives, yet ignore the concepts in his own life? In the five long years since Sigrid's death, he never considered that God was ready for her in heaven. Like Job, he'd questioned the Lord's motives for allowing his beautiful wife to die, but also like Job, he wasn't all knowing. God's ways were mysterious, and He didn't expect Olav to understand them, but He did expect his trust. *Thank You, Father.*

Peace like a warm blanket enveloped him, and he lifted his face to the sky, relishing the heat of the sun on his skin.

"What are you doing, Papa?"

Pivoting toward the voice, he opened his eyes and ruffled Dagmar's hair. "Praising the Lord for His goodness."

"I love God." Her words matter of fact, she slipped her hand into his.

"So do I, honey. So do I." He squeezed her shoulder. "I was coming to get you. We're ready to weed the vegetable garden, and Hazel and I would like your company."

She wrinkled her nose. "Is that a fancy way of saying I'm going to weed, too?"

He chuckled. "You've found me out."

"That's okay. I like working with Hazel. She makes things fun."

"She does indeed." He sauntered back to the garden area, his steps light and springy. "Your assistants are here, *Miss Markham.*"

"Excellent, *Mr. Kristensen.*" Her eyes twinkled as she looked up at them from her position on the ground, and she pointed to the row next to hers. "One of you can start here, and the other can begin at the far end."

"Nope." He motioned for Dagmar to kneel down close by. "We're going to have a race and see who is the fastest."

"You're on!" Hazel crouched over the soil and began to yank out the offending plants. Her hands were a blur as she worked.

Olav snorted a laugh and dropped to his knees. "You're not going to beat me." He jerked the weeds from the ground and chucked them to the side.

"Hey!" In the row next to him, Dagmar waved her hand and coughed. "Keep your mess on your side."

"Sorry." He reached over and brushed the dirt from her dress.

She pushed him away. "Now, you're slowing me down."

He guffawed and turned his attention back to the straggly stalks interspersed with the vegetable plants. Hazel had already moved past him, so he picked up his pace. Moments later, he caught up with her and sent her a wicked grin.

With a giggle, she continued to pull out the unwanted plants and soon progressed ahead of him. She glanced over her shoulder, then pointed behind him. "You're actually supposed to pull *all* the weeds. Speed alone doesn't count."

"You're trying to divert me, but it won't work." He tugged a stem, but the plant remained firmly in the ground. Huffing a breath, he tightened his grip and pulled. The weed came out, and soil and pebbles rained down on him.

"Watch what you're doing!" A clod of dirt hit his chest.

He whipped his head toward Hazel, who also had bits of dirt on her. She wore a broad grin and held another clump in her palm. He tossed the weed at her, and it landed with a thud on her shoulder.

She threw the dirt at him, spraying his shirt.

"This means war!" He growled and crawled toward her, then grabbed her arms. Losing his balance, he tilted, and they fell over onto their sides. Inches from her face, he felt her breath on his cheek. Her pupils dilated, turning her chocolate-brown eyes almost black. His gaze dropped to her lips, pink and perfect. Before he could change his mind, he lowered his mouth on hers.

Chapter Seventeen

Heart pounding against her ribs, Hazel reveled in the feel of Olav's lips on hers. Warm and inviting, his kiss was gentle but not timid. Their breath mingled, and he combed his fingers through her hair. She wrapped her arm around his waist, drawing him closer. Her pulse skittered, and tingles thrummed through her limbs as her toes curled.

How could she be so attracted to him? He was alternately sweet and infuriating. And she'd known him for only a month. Was it possible to fall in love in that short of time?

Love? Was that the emotion coursing through her?

"Papa!"

Olav pulled away and scrambled to his knees. His gaze ricocheted from Dagmar to her. "Dagmar," he stammered. He brushed dirt from his clothing, then picked up his hat and crammed the Stetson onto his head. He swiped at his mouth with the back of his hand.

Cheeks on fire, Hazel sat up and smoothed her skirts. Had her kiss so disgusted him that he had to wipe it off?

"Papa, you were kissing Hazel." Hands on her hips, Dagmar narrowed her eyes. "We're supposed to be working."

"Aren't you the little dictator?" His chuckle sounded forced. "When people are getting married, they kiss. It shows affection, and it's normal."

She cocked her head. "Did you use to kiss Mama?"

Stomach hollow, Hazel stifled a sigh. Once again, Sigrid's presence invaded her world.

"Yes, sweetheart, I did."

"Okay." She shrugged and pointed to the end of her row. "Well, I finished weeding and won the race. What do I get?"

He grabbed her into a bear hug, then lifted her off her feet. She squealed, and he whirled around, making her shriek. "My eternal gratitude. How's that?"

Hazel touched her lips, the memory of his mouth on hers washing over her. She'd responded to his kiss, tugging him toward her like a wanton woman. Her arm had moved of its own volition. Did he think her forward? She had no experience with men. Was it obvious to him?

Ignoring Olav's shenanigans with Dagmar, Hazel collected the discarded weeds into a pile. Why had he kissed her? Until now, it seemed he didn't find her attractive, but when they'd been lying on the ground, so close, his eyes had darkened, and his face had softened. Did he find her pretty? What had changed?

Tears pricked the backs of her eyes. Maybe he was simply lonely. After all, five years had passed since his wife died. Men got lonely. They had needs which was why Mother wouldn't let her be alone with any boys, even when she was too young to understand.

She continued to pile up the discarded plants, the earthy odor of the freshly turned dirt filling her nose. Had he kissed her out of curiosity? He knew she was unmarried, but did he wonder if she'd had experience with men? Would a kiss tell him what he wanted to know? What had her response said?

"Hazel?" Dagmar's voice broke her reverie. "Papa said we're finished here, and we should go for a walk."

Her head whipped up.

Mirror images of each other, Dagmar and Olav stared at her, arms crossed, foreheads wrinkled.

"Oh, uh, of course." She rose and motioned to the pile. "I need to do something with this."

"Leave it. I'll take care of it when we return." He rubbed the back of his neck. "I thought a walk might...uh..."

"Clear the air?"

He glanced at Dagmar, then nodded.

"Fine." She pinned on a smile. "I need to wash up first."

"We all do." He strode to the pump and began to work the handle. Gurgling sounded, and moments later water gushed from the spout, thundering against the ground. She held her hands under the stream, sluicing the dirt from her skin. She stepped back and let Dagmar wash up while she shook the moisture from her fingers. The heat of the day would dry them soon enough.

"All right, ladies, how about we head to the mercantile?" Olav clasped his hands behind his back. "I think some peppermint sticks are in order."

"Yay." Dagmar clapped her hands, then skipped ahead.

"Not too far, Dagmar," he called.

"Yes, Papa."

Hazel smiled as they wandered to the front yard, then through the gate onto the street. The little girl was a delight. Olav had done a superb job of raising her. She had a sweet nature, but like any child, she could be stubborn and unreasonable. Those moments had been few and far between in the month since Hazel had stepped off the train.

Pedestrians lifted their hands in acknowledgment as they passed, some murmuring greetings. More than a few curious looks lingered on her face. Apparently, not everyone knew the preacher had sent for a mail-order bride. What would they think if they knew? How did his congregation feel?

With the exception of the two awful women who'd gossiped the day of the Bible camp celebration, his church members seemed to accept her. Each Sunday, she surreptitiously searched the faces of the attendees, the women in particular, but no one glared at her or avoided her with disdain. They seemed to welcome her into their midst, but how many compared her to Sigrid and secretly found her lacking? Did they resent her absence of Norwegian heritage? Not everyone in the church could claim Scandinavian ancestry, but did they expect it of their pastor's wife?

She caught sight of her reflection in the milliner's window. Wide brown eyes stared back at her, and strands of brown hair straggled out from under her bonnet. Nondescript. And certainly not blonde or fair.

Olav stopped her with a hand on her arm. His gaze pierced her face. "Listen, this is probably not the place to discuss this, but you seem upset. I wanted to say...uh...about the kiss...I'm sorry...I didn't mean to take liberties. I don't want to offend you. My behavior was inappropriate. I want you to know I won't force myself on you. Now, or after we're married. I believe...uh...relations are an expression of feelings for one another, and until we care for each other in that way, I won't expect to consummate the marriage."

Tension slid from her shoulders, and she nodded. "Thank you for telling me that. I didn't know what your expectations were." Would he ever love her as a husband for a wife?

A Family for Hazel

Chapter Eighteen

Was that relief on her face? Did she think him so distasteful that she couldn't imagine a physical relationship? Olav swallowed heavily and stuffed his hands into his pockets. He jerked his head toward Dagmar who waited several doors down in front of the mercantile, her face nearly touching the glass display as her feet fidgeted. "I guess we shouldn't keep her waiting."

Without a word, Hazel whirled and walked to his daughter, then opened the door to the shop, and they headed inside. He pursed his lips as he stared at the vacated space. Pedestrians bumped him as they passed, and he hunched his shoulders into himself.

Would he ever understand his bride-to-be? After an awkward beginning, she'd warmed up to him and Dagmar, especially his daughter. Sharing bits and pieces of her family life and growing-up years, Hazel had given him insight into her character: sweet and full of integrity. He'd finally set aside his belief that she'd stolen from her employer. The jewelry may have been found in her room, but she was not the culprit.

A hand clapped him on the shoulder. "Olav, are you lost?"

He turned and shrugged. "Miles. What are you doing in town?"

"I brought Vanessa to the seamstress, and I'm killing time until she's ready." He cocked his head. "Is everything all right? You seem upset? Has something happened to Dagmar?

"She's fine. Hazel took her into the mercantile."

"That's a relief. Then what's bothering you?" Miles narrowed his eyes. "Struggling with your mail-order bride?"

"How did you know?" Olav frowned. "She's confusing."

"Aren't all women? As much as I love my wife, there are times I can't figure her out. Relationships take time. You've probably forgotten the early days of your first marriage, but I'm sure they weren't all sunshine and roses."

"Hazel is nothing like Sigrid."

"She shouldn't be." Miles motioned to the gazebo that sat in the middle of the park. "Let's not discuss your love life standing in the streets. We'll tell the girls where we are, and they can join us when they're done."

"Well—"

"No argument. You don't want to miss any of my sage wisdom, do you?"

Olav snorted a laugh. "Not for all the *serinakaker* in Green Bay."

With a chuckle, Miles nudged his shoulder, and they made quick work of notifying Hazel where they'd be when she was finished. They sauntered across the street to the park and made their way to the wooden structure on the hill overlooking the bay.

Leaning against the railing, Olav crossed his arms and fixed his gaze on the blue-green water where a stiff breeze created white caps. Behind him, the clatter of wagons and the occasional whinny of a horse punctuated the easy silence that enveloped them. One of the things he appreciated most about his friend was that the man knew when to talk and when to hold his tongue.

Several minutes passed, and Miles cleared this throat. "Finished arguing with yourself?"

Lifting one eyebrow, Olav nodded.

"Look, you thought Hazel would come out here and slip into Sigrid's role without a hiccup, and when she hasn't, you don't know what to do about the situation." Miles held up a hand and touched each finger as he ticked off his comments. "First, as I said, Hazel isn't Sigrid. Nor should she be. Second, she's been here a few weeks. Hardly enough time to have a fully functional relationship. You two barely know what each other's favorite foods are, let alone issues of importance such as how you deal with difficulties or where you stand on certain beliefs."

Olav grunted. The man did make valid points.

"Third, you've been standoffish. I've watched how you interact with her. You're not giving completely of yourself, yet it seems you expect her to do so." Miles's eyes were probing, his mouth turned down. "Not fair, wouldn't you agree?"

"We've been friends a long time, but you couldn't possibly understand."

"Have I been widowed? No, but I know what the Bible says about marriage, and you seem to have forgotten. You also resent being pushed into getting married. A wedding was not in your plans until the elders backed you into it. And now they've pushed up the date. Shed that emotion and thank the Lord for sending a beautiful young woman to be a companion for you and a mother to Dagmar." He jabbed Olav's ribs. "Court the woman. Make her feel special. *Choose* to love her. You don't have to forget Sigrid, or even stop loving her, but Hazel is alive and here now. She deserves your best efforts."

Olav's chest tightened, and he dropped his head. He'd been a selfish oaf. Miles hadn't used those exact words, but his meaning was clear. And he was right.

"Don't beat yourself up too badly, friend." Miles squeezed his arm. "We've all made mistakes. Even me."

"An image shattered." Olav sent him a sly smile. "How will I live with such a revelation."

"Funny." Miles raked his fingers through his hair. "You've got less than two weeks before the circuit preacher comes. Make the most of the time. Lars told me about your conversation with the elders. Vanessa and I would be happy to act as chaperones. Not that you two need watching."

"I kissed her," Olav blurted.

"What?" Miles's eyebrows shot to his hairline. "When?"

"A little while ago. In the garden. We were kidding each other, and one thing led to another..."

"You liked it. I can tell by your expression." Miles guffawed and slapped him on the back. "No wonder you're out of sorts. You didn't expect to enjoy kissing her."

"But I'm not sure she feels the same way." Olav sighed. "I told her it wouldn't happen again, and that seemed to comfort her."

"Well, of course it did. You haven't declared yourself. A woman needs to know she's cared for...loved before accepting your kisses. You've got your work cut out for you, but I've got faith." Miles rubbed his hands together. "Hang on to your spurs, my friend. By the day of your wedding, you'll be running up the aisle to wed Miss Markham."

Olav massaged the back of his neck. Why did life have to be so complicated?

A Family for Hazel

Chapter Nineteen

Hazel took a sip of her water. For the third night in a row, she and Olav had dined with Vanessa and Miles. Conversation ebbed and flowed as Vanessa introduced topics of interest, bringing to mind Mrs. Agnew and her society friends. Her stomach lurched for a moment, then she took a deep breath and pushed away the image.

Hazel peeked at Olav from under her bangs. He was listening to Vanessa describe her idea for a library fundraiser. A smile tugged at one corner of his mouth, and his green eyes crinkled at the corners. His blond hair appeared even lighter against his tanned face.

He'd been acting differently since the day he left her and Dagmar at the mercantile to talk with Miles at the gazebo. If she didn't know any better, she'd think he'd decided to court her. Not that he hadn't been polite before then, but he seemed to take extra care with her, seeking to meet her needs.

What had Miles said to him? Her glance slid to Vanessa's husband, a good-looking man in his own right, but not nearly as handsome as Olav in her estimation. Her groom-to-be wiped his mouth on the napkin, and the memory of his kiss washed over her. Her toes curled as her face burned. Focus, girl!

"Is everything all right, Hazel?" Head cocked, Vanessa stroked her arm. "You look uncomfortable."

"Just a tad warm." She picked up her water glass. "Summers here aren't as hot as at home, but..." She shrugged and drank some water.

"The humidity has been awful the last several days, and the temperatures haven't dropped at night as is typical." Olav's smile grew. "We need a good rain storm to blow away this heat."

"Summers in Virginia were beastly when I lived there." Vanessa sagged against her chair. "I'll take Wisconsin weather any day of the week, but autumn is my favorite season."

"Ja." Olav nodded. "The colors are beautiful, and it's much cooler. I can't wait for you to experience fall. September is almost here."

At which time, she'd be a married woman. How life had changed in the span of a few months. A short time later, dinner was over, and the men had sauntered to the barn to check on one of Miles's mares who was due to foal at any time. He had plenty of staff, including a ranch foreman, but he often saw to the animals himself.

She helped Vanessa clear the table, then pumped water into the sink to wash the dishes.

"Now that the guys are gone, we can have a girl talk." Vanessa patted her back. "And you can tell me how you're doing."

"Okay." She wiped the moisture off a plate, then stacked it in the cupboard. "To be honest, I didn't expect to experience such broad swinging highs and lows. I feel like I'm being blown about like chaff in a wheat field."

"Listen to our East Coast gal talking like a farmer." Vanessa grinned and nudged her shoulder. "Seriously, you've had a lot of changes in a short time, and things haven't exactly gone as planned."

"True, but it's not the adjustments so much as the specter of Olav's wife. She seems to have been a saint, and I think Olav still believes me to be guilty of the stealing charges.

Vanessa barked a laugh. "Sigrid was hardly a saint, but you should talk to Olav about your concerns. You can't begin a marriage with the past overshadowing the present, even though our history does shape us."

"I thought I would escape my past when I moved to Wisconsin, but thanks to the newspapers, that's not the case. I wonder who else read the stories and thinks their pastor is marrying a thief." She dried another plate and put it away. "Will I ever measure up?"

"People are going to believe what they want." Vanessa sighed. "If you recall, I arrived under false pretenses. I've had to live that down, and with God's grace, I've been able to do so for the most part. I've learned that it is up to me to live a life that is pleasing to Him, and the rest will work itself out."

"You make it sound easy."

"Oh, no. Simple, but not easy. A huge difference. Jesus didn't have it easy, and as His followers, we shouldn't expect to either." Vanessa handed her a cup. "Do you honestly think Olav is doubting your innocence, or are you having doubts that you're thrusting onto him?"

Hazel winced. "Good question." What was the answer?

The earthy scent of hay, manure, and animals filled the barn. Snuffling and the occasional whinny sounded as Olav stroked the mare's nose while Miles forked the soiled hay out of the stall and onto a cart. Labor had been quick, and the horse had already cleaned her colt, who wobbled on shaky legs as he searched for milk. "He's beautiful, Miles."

"Ja." He grunted as he hefted another forkful of hay into the dray. "And hopefully he will grow to be big and strong like his father."

"Your stock is some of the healthiest I've ever seen. You're truly blessed."

"As are you." Miles leaned on the tool. "Something is bothering you, my friend. I've watched you with Hazel. You're doing a good job of wooing her."

Olav's face heated. "I feel like a schoolboy in short pants. It's been too long since I've courted."

"It's like riding a horse. You can't have forgotten."

"Perhaps not, but I'm definitely rusty."

"But that's not what's vexing you, is it?"

Leaning on the door, Olav huffed out a loud breath and tugged at his collar. "No."

"I can't help you if you don't tell me what's wrong." He spread clean hay in the stall, patted the mare's flank, and stepped out of the small enclosure. "Walk with me."

They exited the barn. Pinpricks of light dotted the inky blackness of the sky. A fingernail-shaped moon was visible just above the treetops. Birthing the mare had taken longer than he thought. The air was still, expectant.

Sauntering along the lane that led from the barn to the corral, they walked in silence, their boots scuffing the hard-packed earth. A star arced across the darkness, and Olav pressed his lips together. Was God reminding him of His sovereignty?

Miles glanced at him, then leaned on the fence. "You've never cared about what people think. Why has that changed?"

"I keep asking myself that very question. As long as I am pleasing God, people's opinions don't matter. As a pastor, I must live a life above reproach, but He is the one I must answer to, not them."

"You have given this a lot of thought."

"Ja." He rubbed the back of his neck. "But I keep coming back to the situation with Hazel. She, too, must be blameless, without reason for suspicion. I've spoken to the two women who were gossiping about her, but how many of the parishioners know about her past?"

"You need to trust that Miss Milton has done her job in checking Hazel's background. But frankly, I find it suspect that her employer didn't press charges. From the little Hazel has shared with Vanessa, they don't seem the type to forgive and forget. Why didn't they want her punished for her wrongdoing?" He pursed his lips. "She hasn't shared any specifics, but I gather the son is not an honorable man. Fear crept into her eyes the couple of times she referred to her employment. There's something we're missing, and I don't think it's proof that she robbed the Agnews."

"She told me that the jewels were found under her mattress."

"She said as much to Vanessa, but do you think she's foolish enough to hide them there? She's a bright woman. I think she could get away with the act if she set her mind to it."

"But she's never proven she didn't do the deed."

"Because it's her word against theirs." Miles frowned. "And the gentry always come out on top. No one ever believes the servant's word when there is a problem. They're fired after a cursory investigation."

"You're right."

"Of course I'm right." Miles smiled, but quickly sobered. "You need to have a serious and open conversation with Hazel. You need to explain how you feel and listen to her side of things. Then decide once and for all if you are going to set aside your doubts. Or better yet, get those Pinkertons involved. Have them dig into the situation. Find out why the Agnews would claim Hazel stole items if she didn't, and why they didn't press charges if she is guilty." He leveled his gaze at Olav, his teeth flashing in the darkness. "But you must also remember we're all sinners, and she's a redeemed child of God, no matter what she's done. If you don't believe that, you need to revisit your faith and perhaps your position as pastor."

Olav slumped against the fence. He had a long night ahead. Would the Lord leave him with a limp as He'd done with Jacob?

A Family for Hazel

Chapter Twenty

Mouth dry and stomach quivering as if a flock of hummingbirds had taken flight inside, Olav walked down the sidewalk next to Hazel. Setting aside his plans for the day, he'd called on her shortly after breakfast. Despite the heat, she'd agreed to visit the gazebo with him so they would be in view of others and not require a chaperone for their private conversation. He sighed. Sometimes he tired of the constraints of society's rules.

Mottled sunlight peeked through the trees, and the air was thick with moisture. The temperature promised to be scorching by midday. Perspiration trickled down his spine, sticking his shirt to his back. They wandered up the flagstone path and settled on the steps of the wooden structure. He licked his lips. "Are you comfortable?"

"Yes." She rubbed her palms on her skirt as she studied him. "What is this all about? Is everything okay?"

"Ja." He cleared this throat and tried not to think about how the sun's rays caused the highlights in her hair to glisten, creating a halo around her head. "I...uh..." He swallowed, then cleared his throat again.

"You're scaring me, Olav."

"I'm sorry. This is a delicate matter, and I don't want to offend you."

She lifted her hand as if to pat his arm, then drew back.

"Okay." He blew out a loud breath. "I spoke with Miles last night, and he advised me to talk with you once and for all about the situation with your employer."

Her face fell, but she remained silent.

"I want to believe you're innocent, and most times I do, then doubts arise, and I struggle to push them away." He glanced at the sheen of moisture in her eyes. "My words hurt you, but if we're to have a successful marriage, there can be nothing divisive between us. I'm trying to understand why you weren't charged if you were guilty. That makes no sense to me, but I can't ignore the report in the newspaper either."

A single tear tumbled down her cheek, and she swiped it away. Chin trembling, she nodded.

He pulled out his handkerchief and pressed it into her hand. "Your actions since arriving have been without blemish, and your spirit is sweet and gentle. As a pastor...your pastor, I need to accept you as you are, to take you at your word when you say you didn't steal those items." He lowered his head. "But for some reason, at night, alone, I wonder and question."

"As you have every right to do." Her voice was barely above a whisper. "You must think about Dagmar and what sort of example I would be for her. That's what worries you, isn't it?"

"Exactly. She is everything to me, and I couldn't bear it if you turned out to be—"

"Say no more." She straightened her spine and shifted so she was facing him. "I will tell you everything, and then you can decide whether or not I should remain." Her eyes took on a distant stare. "During the war, my parents were part of the Underground Railroad, my father a conductor. Too old to fight, he decided to help the cause by leading escaped slaves to freedom. He made countless trips into Maryland to retrieve people, and one night, he..." Her voice broke, and she pressed her lips together. "He..."

"Take your time," he soothed. "We're in no rush."

Hazel slumped against the upright and blew out a shuddering sigh. "He and the group he was leading were ambushed. We later found out there was a traitor in the Railroad. Fortunately, no one person knew the entire line, so the damage was minimal, but...that didn't bring back my father." She sniffled. "Anyway, two years later Mother was dead. The doctor said influenza, but I know it was a broken heart. She was never the same after he...you know."

Holding his breath, Olav cradled her hand in his. When she didn't pull away, he tightened his grasp.

"Mrs. Agnew was a friend of Mother's, and she offered to take me in, not as a daughter or even a relative, but as a staff member. I didn't have anywhere else to go, so I said yes. I wasn't looking for a handout, and the work helped numb the pain. The servants welcomed me and eventually became like a second family. Mrs. Agnew was nice enough, although a bit aloof, but that's understandable."

"The situation was bearable until about three years ago. Her son, James, took an...um...interest in me. At first, he would sometimes show up in a room I was cleaning. Pop in and say hello or ask me about my day. It seemed harmless, and I enjoyed being able to interact with someone my own age." She stiffened, and her hand flinched in his. "But last summer, he began to corner me, getting close, but not too close. By autumn, he started trying to kiss me, so I tried to work within calling distance of one of the other servants, but it wasn't always possible. I managed to elude him...mostly." Her chin trembled. "Then one night...I don't know when...early January perhaps...he trapped me in one of the parlors and tried....tried—"

"To have his way with you?" Olav's heart pounded, and he gritted his teeth.

Eyes swimming with tears, she nodded. "But I fought back and was able to get away, but as I left the room, he shouted that I would be sorry. He waited for months and stopped badgering me, so I foolishly thought he'd decided to leave me alone. Then he took one of the maids in my room and lifted the mattress to show her the jewelry. He didn't even pretend to search anywhere else. You should have seen the gloating look on his face. He knew he'd won."

"Not for long." Heat flushed Olav's body, and an unquenchable desire to punch the man swept over him. "This may not be the first time he's been inappropriate with staff. I'm going to contact the Pinkerton Agency and start them on an investigation into this beast, to prove he framed you and that he tried to force himself on you and perhaps other women." He kissed the back of her hand. "And I hope you'll forgive me for not addressing this sooner, for not asking your side of the story, and for jumping to conclusions."

She gave him a wobbly smile. "Of course, I forgive you."

His heart swelled at her trust-filled gaze. He would ensure justice was served and do everything in his power to keep her looking at him as she did at this moment.

A Family for Hazel

Chapter Twenty-One

Dust motes flew into the air as Hazel swept the sanctuary floor. Perspiration pooled under her arms and formed at her hairline in the hot confines of the church. The windows were open, but the air outside was still. No cool breeze provided relief. Across the room Vanessa created a multi-colored flower arrangement for the altar. Miles and Olav were in one of the rooms down the hall repairing a doorframe. If she strained, she could hear the rumble of their deep voices punctuated by the ring of a hammer.

After yesterday's conversation with Olav at the gazebo, the heaviness that she'd carried with her from Pennsylvania was finally gone from her chest. She'd slept through the night, awakening this morning refreshed and at peace. Initially embarrassed by her tears, she'd rested in his assurances that she had every right to grieve the loss of her parents even after so many years. The spark in his eyes when he spoke of James attested to Olav's anger on her behalf. He shared her burden.

Her pulse thrummed at the memory of his thumb rubbing circles on the back of her hand entwined in his. They'd sat in companionable silence, shoulders touching, for nearly thirty minutes after he'd finished outlining his plan to make James pay for his subterfuge and repair her tarnished reputation. More importantly, he believed her innocent. His expression was no longer shadowed by doubt about her integrity.

She lifted her right hand and studied the skin. Smooth like always, but changed because of the kiss he'd laid there after dropping her off at the boarding house. She blew out a breath and shook her head. The work wouldn't get done if she continued to moon about like a schoolgirl. With a broad smile, she resumed sweeping.

"I've never seen someone so happy to clean." Vanessa smirked at her from a few yards away. "Do you find the task so exciting as to be giddy about doing it?"

Hazel's cheeks heated, and she giggled. "I'm not giddy."

"Seems so from here." Vanessa carried the vase to the front and set it on the carved wooden table behind the pulpit. She turned and wiggled her eyebrows. "But perhaps there's another reason for your joyful mood."

"Olav and I spoke at great length yesterday. I told him everything, and he's going to secure the services of the Pinkertons. He no longer questions my guilt." She shrugged. "It feels good to have his support, that's all. We're no longer at odds."

"Uh-huh." Vanessa crossed her arms, a smug look on her face. "I'm fairly certain it's more than that. I think someone is beginning to fall in love with her handsome Norwegian groom-to-be."

Pulse skittering, Hazel tightened her grasp on the broom handle. Her breath caught, and her jaw dropped as she stared at her friend. She couldn't possibly be in love. It was too soon. Besides, Olav would never love her back, not that way. She couldn't afford to lose her heart to him while he still adored his late wife. "Nonsense. No one falls in love in a month."

Snorting a laugh, Vanessa grabbed her hands and pulled her into a quick hug. "The lady doth protest too much, methinks."

"I'm just happy that we're getting along so much better."

"Let's review the bidding. You're grinning like a cat who finished a full bowl of cream, and totally distracted. Your eyes search for him whenever you enter a room where he might be. And if I'm not mistaken, you were listening for the sound of his voice when you had your head tilted." She chuckled and pointed to Hazel's face. "And just talking about him brings a lovely pink color to your cheeks. Bet your pulse is doing the polka right this very minute."

Hazel burst out laughing. "Okay, you're right...well, not that I'm necessarily in love, but I like him. A lot. He makes me feel things...strange things. Since yesterday, I think about him all the time. How can my emotions do such a turnabout?"

"That's why it's called *falling* in love." Vanessa squeezed her shoulder. "I'm thrilled for you and Olav. You've both had a difficult life. You deserve to find happiness. "Now, go grab him and Miles so we can move the cabinet back to the Sunday school room."

"Yes, ma'am." Hazel put two fingers to her forehead in a mock salute and hurried from the room, Vanessa's giggle following her down the hall. She forced herself to slow down, then tugged at her bodice and patted her hair. She pushed open the door that led to the backyard where the men were supposed to be weeding the gardens, but the grassy area was vacant. "Miles? Olav?" Craning her neck, she peered into the trees at the back of the property searching for movement. Nothing.

Lifting her skirts, she picked her way across the lawn, then stopped at the sound of her name as Olav's voice sounded from inside the building. "I wish Hazel felt better about herself. That debacle with the Agnews really did a number on her confidence."

"Show her how you feel, and under your care, she will blossom."

"But what if she never grows to love me as much as I love her."

Hazel clapped a hand over her mouth. He *loved* her? Or was he telling Miles what he thought his friend wanted to hear?

Olav swallowed and rubbed the back of his neck. "It didn't feel like this with Sigrid, and that scares me."

"A little fear is good." Miles chuckled and clapped him on the back. "You're older now, more mature. I'm not an expert at love, but people change, develop. Why wouldn't their ability to love do the same?" He crossed his arms. "And before you say anything else, this doesn't mean you loved Sigrid less, just differently."

"I don't know." The room was stifling, and sweat sprang out on his forehead and above his lips. He tugged at his collar, then walked to the window and shoved the casement higher. No refreshing breeze filtered through the opening. He huffed a breath and pivoted on his heel. "Why can't I get a handle on this?"

"You're in uncharted waters. You hadn't planned to remarry, let alone care for another woman. The situation was thrust on you, and if you're like most people, you don't like being painted into a corner." Miles leaned against the wall. "But look on this as a good thing. God has given you another chance at happiness. I didn't expect to love Vanessa, especially after discovering she came under false pretenses, but the Lord was able to clear away all the rubbish between us, and we have a full and joyful marriage."

Olav huffed out a loud sigh and raked his fingers through his hair. "I'm crippled with guilt. My head knows that Sigrid wouldn't want me to be alone, and she'd be thrilled that Dagmar will have a mother, but part of my heart clenches at the thought of having feelings for someone else. Like I'm being disloyal."

"Have you prayed about this, old man?"

"Yes. No. Well, honestly, not as I should."

"Trying to work this one out on your own, are you?" Miles grinned. "And you see where that's gotten you."

"You're not helping. You realize that, right?"

Miles grasped his shoulders, his gaze piercing. "All kidding aside, Olav, you've been given a wonderful opportunity. You're the theologian, but I don't think your heavenly Father would allow you to fall in love with

Hazel if she didn't either already love you or will grow to do so. He wants to give you an abundant life, and I don't know that He handpicks all men's wives, but in this case I think He has. You've only been courting her a short time. Give it time."

"But we're to wed in only a few days."

"And Lord willing, you'll have a lifetime to shower her with love, to convince her that you're worthy of her love."

Olav's stomach hollowed. He pulled away from Miles and returned to the window. Staring out the glass pane, he nibbled his lower lip. God had taken Sigrid. Would He be willing to give him a lifetime with Hazel? Or would He snatch her away, too?

"Don't go there, Olav."

"Go where?" Olav whirled and shoved his hands into his pockets. "Ask whether God will see fit not to make me a widower for a second time? To shatter my heart with another loss?"

"None of us is assured one more day, but we can't refuse to open ourselves up because of fear."

"But—"

Miles held up his hands as if in surrender. "I have not walked in your shoes, but I think you'll regret it if you turn your back on God's gift." A smirk broke out on his face. "Besides, I see how she looks at you. She's on her way to falling in love with you, if she hasn't already."

Footsteps sounded in the corridor, then Hazel appeared in the doorway, a tentative smile curving her lips. How much, if any, of the conversation had she heard?

A Family for Hazel

Chapter Twenty-Two

Two days later, Hazel entered the mercantile with Dagmar. Seemingly overnight, the child had outgrown her clothes, and the dress she was to wear to the wedding no longer fit. Distraught, the little girl claimed she couldn't attend the event, so Hazel assured her they had enough time to make a new garment.

Grateful for the opportunity to do something for Dagmar and hold her own nervousness about the upcoming nuptials at bay, she walked to the back of the shop where bolts of fabric lined two shelves.

Mrs. Calhoun, who owned the shop with her husband, hurried toward them with a smile. "Miss Markham, how lovely to see you again. What brings you in for a visit?"

Hazel wrapped her arm around Dagmar's shoulder. "This young lady needs a new dress, and I'm hoping you are able to help us."

The older woman clapped her hands. "Ah, yes, for your upcoming wedding, no doubt." She walked behind the counter and yanked three bolts of material from the shelf: pastel yellow, blue, and pink. "With her beautiful coloring, I think these might do the trick." And the cotton weave will be nice and cool. She leaned over and pinched Dagmar's cheek. "Do any of them meet your fancy?"

The youngster rolled her eyes toward Hazel in a silent plea for help.

"They are very pretty, but if I'm not mistaken, her favorite color is purple." Hazel lowered one eyelid in a slow wink at Dagmar. "Perhaps you have something in lavender?"

A shadow danced across the woman's face for a second, then her expression brightened. "Of course." She shoved the bolts to the side, then ran her finger along the rainbow of fabric on the shelves.

Hazel stifled the urge to push her aside and yank out the two light-purple rolls on the top shelf. Was the woman making a point of some sort? She'd been welcoming upon their arrival, but was she offended that Olav's daughter had other preferences? Finally, the shopkeeper reached overhead and selected the material Hazel had spied.

"What do you think about either of these, honey?" Ignoring Hazel, Mrs. Calhoun leaned toward Dagmar.

With a glance at Hazel, the little girl poked her finger at the orchid-colored material with tiny white flowers.

"Perfect," Hazel and Mrs. Calhoun exclaimed in unison.

Dagmar grinned. "Now, can I pick out a peppermint stick?"

"Not much for shopping?" Hazel giggled.

Wrinkling her nose, the child shook her head. "Not really. Papa doesn't like it either."

"I'll keep that in mind." She turned and looked at Mrs. Calhoun. "We'll take five yards, and all the associated notions."

"I'll put it on Pastor Kristensen's tab." The woman measured and cut the fabric, then began to pull together the thread, needles, and other items Hazel would need to create the outfit. "I assume you already have a dress?"

"Yes, thank you." Her mind went to the simple beige dress among her belongings. Two years old, it had held up well, but should she have purchased or made something new? She'd come West out of desperation, believing it wouldn't matter what she wore for her wedding. A marriage of convenience didn't need fancy clothes, did it?

The bell jangled at the front door, and Olav strode inside.

"Papa!" Dagmar threw her arms around his waist. "We got peppermint sticks."

He chuckled, the sound warm and rumbling in his chest. He kissed the tip of her nose, then lifted his gaze to Hazel. "Apparently, the most important of today's purchases."

Hazel knees quivered, and she gripped the counter to keep from pitching over. Goodness, but he looked handsome today. His green shirt was a shade darker than his eyes, and his jacket molded to his shoulders as if tailor-made. His sun-bleached blond hair contrasted with his tanned face. "Apparently." The word came out breathless. Did he hear that?

"Are you finished?" His glance slid from Hazel to Mrs. Calhoun, who seemed quite interested in their exchange. "I've got...information."

With a nod, she picked up her reticule and reached for the brown paper package tied with twine.

He took it from her, then extended his elbow, and Hazel slipped her hand in the crook of his arm. "Then we're off. Can you grab Dagmar's hand? I thought we'd stop by the park on the way home." He dipped his head at the shopkeeper. "Thank you for helping my girls, Mrs. Calhoun."

"Always a pleasure, Pastor, always a pleasure." She minced across the floor behind them, then gave an animated wave as they headed outside.

They walked in silence, and Hazel perused the displays in the shop windows as they passed. Green Bay had more than a few high-end stores. Moments later they arrived at the verdant square dotted with gardens. "Stay away from the water, Dagmar. We'll be over here." He motioned to a wooden bench a few yards away.

"Yes, Papa." Sucking on the peppermint stick, she wandered toward a flower bed overflowing with roses.

His eyes followed her for several minutes, then he turned toward Hazel, and they sat down. "Thank you for offering to make her a new dress. We could have made alterations to the other one."

"I'm happy to do it. Every woman wants to look her best at a special event, even one who is eight years old."

"Still, it means a lot."

"You're welcome." She licked her lips. "Now, you have news? What did you find out?"

Excitement danced across his face, and his eyes sparkled. "You're not going to believe this...well, maybe you will. Anyway, your Mrs. Agnew has hired three girls to fill your position. Each one has lasted only a couple of weeks. Pinkertons hasn't found them to interview, but arrangements were made so that one of their operatives was the only applicant after the most recent maid left. The agent just started yesterday."

"A spy?" Hazel gaped at him. "Can they do that?"

He shrugged. "I guess so. They also discovered that James has managed to get himself put on every one of his mother's bank accounts. And has sold his house and moved in with her. Seems shady to me."

"He has expensive tastes and is probably running out of money. I'm not sure why he hasn't married some heiress yet, unless they're smarter than I think, and see who he really is."

"Pinkertons made great progress in a short time. With luck, this will be resolved by the wedding, which I'm looking forward to." He squeezed her hand, then pulled a small box from his pocket. His faced pinked. "It's not much, but I hope you like it."

Her fingers fumbled with the wrapping paper, and a nervous laugh bubbled up. She finally tore away the decorative covering to reveal a small, walnut wood frame. "Thank you. It's beautiful." Her face fell. "But I didn't get you anything."

"You don't have to. I saw this at the stationers and thought perhaps you'd want to put our wedding photo in it."

"Ja...I mean yes."

His laughter rang out. "Now, you're getting it."

Warmth spread from her stomach to the tips of her hands and feet. Her toes curled as she beamed at him. She never wanted this feeling to go away. She would make him love her if it was the last thing she did.

Chapter Twenty-Three

Humming her favorite hymn, Hazel finished frosting the chocolate cake, its sweet aroma filling her nose. Behind her, Vanessa was making potato salad, and Dagmar was on the couch with a book. The men were outside, having made excuses about being in the way. Sunlight filtered through the windows, and a light breeze cooled the kitchen.

Hazel stepped back and inspected the cake with satisfaction. Perfect. Movement outside caught her attention, and she craned her neck to watch. Several yards away, Olav and Miles stood near the vegetable garden talking. She couldn't hear the words, but they were deep in conversation. Then Olav threw back his head and laughed, holding his stomach. Miles looked smug.

She studied the two who, were so alike, yet so different, and equally handsome. Whereas both were blond and deeply tanned, Miles had blue eyes, and Olav's were green. She didn't know for certain, but Olav probably stood six feet, his friend towering over him by a few inches, but it was her groom-to-be that set her heart pumping when he walked into the room. Or when she caught a glimpse of him.

With a sigh, she wiped her hands on the towel, then turned.

Vanessa wore the same smirk Hazel had seen on Miles. "Enjoying the view?"

Cheeks warm, Hazel shrugged. "I don't know what you're talking about."

"Right. We can play that game." Vanessa winked and stirred the potato salad. "I'm done here. What else do we need to prepare for dinner?"

"The roast is in the oven, and I'll cook the green beans a few minutes before we sit down for the meal."

"Excellent. Sounds like a great time for some coffee and conversation." Vanessa jerked her head toward the door. "Inside or out?"

"How about on the porch?" Hazel went to the couch. "Dagmar, Miss Vanessa and I are going to sit outside and chat. Would you like to join us?"

The little girl looked up. "Do I have to?"

"Not at all." Hazel smiled. "You love to read, don't you?"

"Yes, and I'm just getting to the good part. The princess is being chased by the goblins."

"Sounds exciting." She ran her fingers through Dagmar's hair, then patted the child's shoulder. "Have fun and stay away from the stove. Holler if you need anything."

Head buried in the pages, the youngster mumbled a response.

A pair of mugs filled with steaming coffee in her hands, Vanessa waited by the open door.

Hazel crossed the room, and they walked outside. She squinted against the sun's glare and lowered herself in one of the wooden rocking chairs. Varnished to a high sheen, the rocker creaked with each move, a comforting sound that brought to mind firefly-filled nights on the veranda in Pennsylvania before the war when she and her parents would sit for hours starring at the constellations and sipping lemonade. An amateur astronomer, her father would point out his favorite stars, and she'd feign interest. All the points of light looked the same to her, but the important part was spending time with him.

Then the war happened, and he was gone.

Her grip tightened on the mug, and the heat scorched her palm, the pain on her hands siphoning off some of the ache in her heart.

"Are you okay?" Vanessa's forehead was wrinkled. "You seem upset."

"Memories. Bittersweet."

Vanessa set her mug on the ground next to the chair, then squeezed Hazel's arm. "Do you want to talk about them? Just because you've begun a new chapter in your life doesn't mean you've left behind your old life."

"Thanks, but no." Hazel waved her hand. "Another time, perhaps. The rockers creak like the ones at home."

"Ah, yes. Sounds and smells evoke the strongest memories for me." She picked up her coffee and sipped the dark brew. "For me, it's the sound of the whippoorwill and the smell of rose water. The woman who stole my lowdown, no-good, cheating fiancé wore the stuff, and the birds sounded outside my bedroom window the night I caught them together. It's not the poor birds' fault, but I can't stand to hear them, even though I'm better off without Frederick."

"How awful."

"Like I said, I'm better off, but my bruised pride sometimes smarts." She huffed out a breath. "But enough about me. Let's talk about the upcoming festivities. Only three days, and you'll be a married woman. How's Dagmar's dress coming?"

"Nearly finished. I used a simple pattern. I need to hem the sleeves and skirt, and put on the buttons."

"Goodness, you're fast."

"I did a lot of sewing as a young lady." Another memory washed over her in which she stood near her mother and packed a satchelful of freshly made clothes for another group of escaped slaves. "We provided a lot of clothing to those in need."

"I'm a terrible seamstress." Vanessa giggled. "You'd be appalled at my stitches."

"You have other gifts." Hazel smiled at her over the edge of her mug. "Like making new people feel welcome."

"It is one of her gifts."

Hazel whipped her head around.

Miles and Olav ascended the stairs onto the porch, and Miles went to his wife and placed a kiss on her head. "One of the many traits that drew me to her."

"Eventually," Vanessa scoffed. "It took us a while to get our bearings."

"And now look at you lovebirds." Olav grinned. "An example for every young couple at church."

"Papa!" Dagmar burst out of the house, her eyes wide. "Papa! I can't find my locket."

"What?" He caught his daughter in his arms, then squatted in front of her. "The locket Mama gave you?"

"Yes." I was reading my book, and I wanted to be like the princess, so I thought if I put on my necklace, I would be pretty like her. And I can't find it."

"Where did you have it last? Did you check your nightstand?"

Olav looked over her head at Hazel, his eyes clouded.

A cold wave of nausea swept over Hazel, and she stared at Olav. This couldn't be happening again. A lost piece of jewelry while she was in the house. She could see suspicion edging its way into his expression. Even after their conversations, and his claim that he believed she had nothing to do with Mrs. Agnew's jewels found under her mattress, doubt was taking hold of him.

"I see it on your face. You think I took her necklace, don't you?" She jumped to her feet, hands trembling. "Why would I do that? It's a child's trinket, and it's not like I could ever wear it."

"No." He licked his lips.

A sure sign he was lying. Hazel clenched her fists. "I am not a thief, but you're never going to believe me." She fumbled with the ties of her apron, then managed to untangle them and yank off the garment. She tossed it on the chair, tears falling, and said, "I can't do this." She raced down the steps, pushed open the gate, and ran down the street.

So much for making Olav love her.

Chapter Twenty-Four

His stomach a cold pit, Olav gaped at Miles and Vanessa, then rushed after Hazel. Pushing through the pedestrians, he searched for her cinnamon-colored hair among the bonnets and hats. Nothing. At the next intersection, he looked left, then right. Both streets were vacant. Eerily vacant. Where had Hazel gone? Should he run up and down the road searching for her? Knock on doors? She didn't want to be found. His efforts would be futile.

Trudging back to the house, he raked his fingers through his hair. In the span of a few seconds, he'd ruined everything. He had never been good at hiding his thoughts and emotions, and he knew she'd seen the doubt on his face. The niggling mistrust that had surfaced as soon as Dagmar said her necklace was missing. All his claims of believing in Hazel were empty words. At the first sign of difficulty, he'd failed her. No wonder she'd fled.

He dropped onto the couch and leaned his head against the back cushion. Closing his eyes, he blew out a deep breath, but the tightness in his chest remained. The silence in the room was thick, and he dared not open his eyes to look at his friends. Or maybe he should, so he could see the censure on their expressions he deserved.

"Papa?" Dagmar nestled next to him and tugged at his sleeve. "Papa? Why did Miss Hazel run away?"

"Because Papa messed up." Olav sat up and pulled his daughter onto his lap, tucking her head under his chin. "He hurt her feelings."

"How did you do that?"

"It's a long story, honey." He frowned at Miles who had sat down in a nearby chair. Vanessa busied herself in the kitchen, probably hoping her husband would rebuke him. Did he need to hear what he already knew? That he didn't deserve Hazel or any woman. And he certainly didn't deserve to be pastor of a church.

"Are you finished?" Miles cocked his head. "I'll wait."

"Finished what?"

"Beating yourself up and thinking Hazel is too good for you." He chuckled. "No, I'm not a mind reader. I've been in your shoes."

Olav cradled Dagmar closer, his arms wrapped snugly around her small frame. "I'm such an oaf. I believe she's innocent. With all my heart, I know that to be true, yet somehow, for a split second, I was filled with suspicion. It was out there before I could grab it back." His throat thickened, and he swallowed the lump that formed. "I am a terrible man. No woman should have to live with me. And I should probably resign my position."

"Whoa." Miles lifted one hand. "Hold on for a moment. Is this serious? Yes, and we'll do our best to help you find Hazel and make things right. And with God's grace and mercy, they will be, but there is no reason for you to leave the church. Do you think you're the only person to make a mistake, to sin in his heart? Hardly."

"But how can I minister to people if I can't do as I should?"

"What does Paul say in the book of Romans—that which I hate, I do?" He quirked an eyebrow. "We're all imperfect, my friend, and we're going to mess up. That doesn't mean you can't serve the Lord or have a happy, loving marriage to Hazel."

"May I say something?" Vanessa strode across the room and stood behind Miles. "I don't want to speak out of turn."

"Never fear that." Olav pursed his lips. "We've known each other long enough not to stand on ceremony. But go easy on me."

"I believe you haven't shed your guilt over remarrying and are looking for any reason not to wed Hazel." She raised her shoulder in a delicate shrug. "I can't imagine the pain you feel at losing Sigrid, but she would want you to be happy, to find love again. Even the Bible says it's okay to marry again."

Dagmar turned in his lap until she faced him. Putting a hand on either side of his face, she narrowed her eyes. "Miss Vanessa is right, Papa. I don't remember much about Mama, but I think she wouldn't want you to be sad and lonely. And if you marry Miss Hazel you won't be.

She's nice and fun and makes me feel like a big girl. I love her as my new mama. Why can't you love her, too?"

"I do love her, Dagmar."

"Then why do you keep upsetting her? You shouldn't do that."

He chuckled, and his breath caught. Out of the mouth of babes. He exchanged glances with Miles and Vanessa. Could he repair his relationship to Hazel? Could they start over again even after all he'd done?

"Seems like we need to ask for help." She laid her hand on Miles's arm. "Would you pray for us, honey?"

"I think I should do that." Olav grimaced. "I need to ask forgiveness before anything else is said." Miles and Vanessa nodded, and Olav silently thanked God for their friendship. He cleared his throat, then tucked Dagmar at his side, clasping one of her tiny hands in his. Closing his eyes, he prayed, "Dear Father, forgive my selfishness and stupidity. I've hurt one of Your children, a woman I love very much. Thank You for sending her to me. Help me find her so I can apologize and assure her of my love and acceptance. Work in her heart that she might grant me a pardon I don't deserve."

Like a blanket on a cold winter's night, peace settled over him. "Thank You, God." He opened his eyes and swiped at the tears that had come unbidden.

Dagmar reached up and kissed his cheek. "Everything will work out, Papa. You'll see."

"I hope you're right, little one, I hope you're right."

Chapter Twenty-Five

Heart racing, Hazel yanked open the door of the boarding house and raced up the stairs, her feet pounding on the treads. If alive, her mother would be appalled at her actions: running through the streets, making the pins fall from her hair and causing the tresses to stream down her back, and galloping up the steps.

But that was the whole problem. Mother was dead, forcing Hazel to find refuge with the Agnews. The despicable family who ruined her life. A sob burst from her lips, and she pressed her hand against her mouth.

The aroma of beef stew filled the house. Normally one of her favorite meals, the smell caused her stomach to roil, and she swallowed against the wave of nausea that threatened to overwhelm her. A door cracked in the corridor, and the newest tenant peeked out. Hazel ducked her head and rushed to her room. Her hands shook as she tried to jam the key into the knob. She finally managed to unlock the door, and she pushed her way inside.

Olav hadn't followed her. Did that mean he was through with her? Or would he show up with Sheriff Baas demanding that the lawman arrest her? She had to get out of Green Bay.

"But where can I go?" Her voice broke as she opened the armoire and pulled out her satchels. She couldn't carry her trunk, but she'd take as much as she could stuff in the bags. From the bureau drawers, she pulled her underthings, then moved to the wardrobe and selected a handful of bodices and two skirts.

Hazel surveyed the room to determine what else she should take, and her eyes fell on her Bible on the nightstand. Her chin trembled. "How could you let this happen, God?" She picked up the leather-bound volume and stroked the cover. A gift from her parents on her twelfth birthday, it was one of the few personal items she'd brought from Pennsylvania. She might never read it again, but she couldn't leave it behind.

Footsteps sounded in the hallway, and she held her breath, her pulse skittering. A door banged shut, then silence.

She sucked in a deep breath. Must hurry. She shoved the Bible into the top of the bag, then closed the latch. Catching sight of herself in the mirror over the dresser, she grimaced. "Pull yourself together, Hazel." She picked up her brush and dragged it through her hair, then pinned the locks into a bun at the base of her neck. She'd left her hat at Olav's, so her bonnet would have to do. She tied it onto her head, slipped a shawl from the hook, and draped it around her shoulders. She tucked her toiletries into the second bag and fastened it.

"One last thing." She pulled a sheet of paper and pen from the desk drawer, then unscrewed the ink bottle, and dipped the nib into the ink. She scribbled a hasty letter to her landlady apologizing for her quick departure and giving instructions to contact Vanessa to dispose of her remaining clothes. Perhaps there was a needy woman in town who could use them. She propped the note in front of the mirror, then rummaged in her reticule for some coins. She laid the money near the note and picked up her luggage with a grunt. Good thing she was used to hard work. The bags were heavier than she'd anticipated.

"Best get on with it." She exited the room, leaving the door ajar, then hurried down the stairs and out of the house. Still no sign of Olav. Proof he was glad to be rid of her. She blinked away the tears pricking the backs of her eyes and straightened her spine. Perhaps with enough time, her shattered heart would heal, but was she destined to be alone the rest of her life?

She thought she'd finally found a family, but once again it had been ripped from her hands. Would she ever have the chance to marry? Could she find a man to trust and cherish her? To provide for her? To give her the children she desired?

Pushing her way through the pedestrians, she shook her head. No. She was destined to be a spinster, looked at with pity. Maybe there was an orphanage where she could obtain a job. They could be her family. A poor substitute but better than nothing.

Chest heaving from exertion, she made it to the train station, then to the window, and set the satchels at her feet. Conversation ebbed and flowed around her, and shouts from the platform filtered through the building. "One second-class ticket to Wausau, please."

Grizzled and gray haired, the man nodded and slipped her the stub. "You'd best hurry, young lady; the train leaves in three minutes."

"Thank you." She poked the ticket into her reticule, lifted her bags, and pushed her way through the throng to the platform toward the train. A dark-skinned porter smiled at her, and she sighed. Her escape was imminent.

"I take yo' bags for you, ma'am." He reached for the luggage. "They look awfully heavy."

"Thank you. I'm in second class. Can you help me?"

"Yes'm." Carrying her satchels as if they weighed no more than loaves of bread, he climbed into the nearest passenger car.

She took one last look around and followed him inside. Half filled, the car had upholstered benches and a wooden floor. Brass sconces hung from the walls. Some of the windows were open, allowing the steam from the locomotive to drift inside.

He gestured to a bench near a woman with three children. "How's dat?"

"Perfect." She sighed. The sight of the little ones tugged at her heart, but sitting near them would be better than fighting off potential interest from a man. Safer, too. After he tucked her bags under the bench, she pressed a coin into his hand. "Thank you for your help. You've been most kind."

Touching his brim with two fingers, his face lit up. "It be my pleasure."

Hazel sank into the seat and nodded to the woman. Would the train ever get going?

Breath ragged in his ears, Olav ran to the train station. After leaving Dagmar with Miles and Vanessa, he'd made his way to Hazel's boarding house to discover she'd left. For good. Her landlady showed him the note, glaring at him as if she knew he was the reason his bride-to-be had fled. He'd thanked her, then dashed from the house, feet clattering.

The train whistle shrieked, and he pushed himself to run faster, a cramp clutching his side. *Please, God, hold the train.* He pushed past a sauntering couple, then leapt over a dog lounging on the sidewalk. The station came into view, and with a burst of speed, he crossed the street and sprinted the last few yards across the nearly vacant platform to the hulking vehicle that had begun to chug its way down the track.

"No!" He waved his hands and darted forward.

An ebony-skinned porter gripped the rail of the caboose with one hand and held out his other. "Sir!"

Feet pounding against the wood, Olav surged forward, his fingers straining to make contact with the man's. Reaching. Reaching.

The porter leaned out farther, wrapped his palm around Olav's arm in a vise-like grip, and dragged him onto the bottom step of the car.

Body trembling like a branch on a blustery day, Olav stumbled up the last two steps, then fell at the man's feet. "Thank you," he gasped.

The man squatted next to him and patted his shoulder. "You be looking for the brown-haired woman with the sad eyes?"

"Yes, how—"

"You ain't the first guy to chase down one of my trains." He flashed a grin at Olav and stood. "And you probably won't be the last. You best get to it. We'll be in Wausau in a couple of hours, and you got some apologizin' to do."

"You're a wise man." Olav struggled to his feet. "Wiser than me."

"Nah. Jus' seen a lot in my years on the railroad." He shrugged. "She be two cars up."

"Thanks." Olav dug into his pocket, pulled out several coins, and pressed them into the man's hand. Without another word, he open the door and hurried through the first compartment between him and the love of his life. He knew that now, but would he be able to convince her. He went through the next car, then hesitated on the junction platform, his body swaying in rhythm with the rocking of the train. *Give me the words, Lord. Without Your help, I'm sure to mess this up.*

He squared his shoulders and marched through the door. His gaze ricocheted from face to face. Then he saw her. Face pale, and eyes red rimmed, she stared at him, her mouth forming a perfect O. Before he could lose his nerve, he traversed the aisle, then motioned to the empty space beside her. "May I join you?"

Her mouth worked, but nothing came out, and she nodded. A sheen of moisture covered her eyes. Her lovely, deep-chocolate eyes.

His breath whooshed out, and he lowered himself onto the bench. One small victory. She hadn't had him thrown off the train.

She scooted away from him and pulled her skirts close. "What are you doing here," she hissed.

He stifled the desire to take her into his arms and shower kisses on her face, begging her forgive him. Instead, he clenched his hands in his lap and gazed into her eyes. "I came to apologize and tell you what a fool I've been. I don't deserve another chance to prove myself to you, but I hope you'll give me the grace to try."

Her eyes widened, and uncertainty clouded her face, but she shook her head. "Why should I believe you? You obviously still don't trust me. You said you did, but at the first sign of trouble, you thought I was the culprit."

"I know, and I'm an idiot. We found the necklace. It had fallen behind Dagmar's dresser onto the floor." He tugged at his collar. "I have no right to ask this of you, but will you please forgive me for all the hurt I've caused?"

A little boy poked his head over the bench, his front two teeth missing. "What'd you do, mister?"

Olav reared back. "Uh, I thought she stole something, but she didn't."

"That's not very nice. You should say you're sorry."

"I'm trying to."

Beside him, Hazel released a soft giggle. Was there hope for them?

"Timmy. Sit down and leave those people alone." The boy's mother sent Olav an apologetic smile.

"It's all right, ma'am. I'm making a fool of myself in public; he has every right to ask what's going on." Olav climbed to his feet and held out his arms. "Anyone else curious? I'll tell you what I did. I ruined the chance for happiness with this beautiful woman because I was a fool, and a boor. I'm running out of words to describe my poor behavior. She entrusted her heart to me, and I crushed it by believing ill of her. I love her with every fiber of my being, and I might lose her because of my actions."

"You love me?" Hazel gawked at him. "But what about Sigrid?"

A lump formed in his throat, and he swallowed. "Yes, I love you. Sigrid will always hold a special place in my heart, but she is gone, and my life is with you now...if you'll have me." He went down on one knee. "Will you do me the honor of being my wife, not because the elders say so or because propriety demands it, but because you might have the smallest of feelings for me. Because you care for this flawed, foolish man who would like to start over. I promise to spend the rest of my life making up for my mistakes, ensuring you know how special you are—"

Hazel pressed her fingers against his mouth. "I love you, too. More than just a little. Thank you for coming after me. We have a lot to work out, but I want to do it together."

"Then you'll marry me." He spoke through her fingers.

"Yes." Tears tumbled down her cheeks. "Yes," she repeated.

With a whoop, he jumped to his feet, then gripped the back of the bench to keep from pitching to the floor. "Did you hear that? She said yes."

Applause broke out as he pulled her into an embrace. He pressed his lips on hers, a kiss filled with love and promise.

A Family for Hazel

One year later

Epilogue

The locomotive thundered into the Green Bay station, and steam enveloped the throng waiting the iron behemoth's arrival. Flanked by Dagmar and Olav, Hazel gripped their hands as her heart fluttered. Tiny faces appeared in the windows of the passenger cars. Their little boy was here. What would he look like? Would he grow to love them, or would he resent his relocation from New York City?

Several months ago, she'd seen an article in the *Green Bay Gazette* about Reverend Charles Brace's work with children who had lost their parents for one reason or another, or been given up by a mother or father who could no longer care for them. Rather than house the little ones in overcrowded asylums and orphanages in the city, he'd come up with the idea to send them to the Midwest to families who could give them fresh air and a fresh start. His program had been operating for nearly twenty-five years and had seen much success.

"Relax." Olav leaned over and kissed her cheek. His eyes caressed her, and he squeezed her fingers. "The letter from the Children's Aid Society said Henri was excited about coming to live with us. And he's going to love you."

Her pulse jumped. Even after a year of marriage, Olav's touch sent shivers thrumming up her spine. After lots of discussion and hard work, they'd laid aside their mistrust and hurt feelings, and their relationship was sweet and strong. He had given away most of Sigrid's things to needy families within the community, but Hazel insisted the quilts and other items she had made remain so that Dagmar could choose whether or not to keep them.

Brakes squealed, and the train ground to a halt. Moments later, children of all sizes streamed down the steps and onto the platform. The younger children were led by adults or older kids. Trepidation was etched on most faces.

"The poor darlings seem terrified." Tears sprang to Hazel's eyes. "I didn't think about what it must be like to be put on a train and taken from everything familiar."

"We'll pray for them as they adjust to their new lives." Olav let go of her hand and wrapped his arm around her waist. "Fortunately, the people who are here to take in the children are looking to expand their families, not obtain workers. I've heard that's sometimes the case. Farmers need help with their properties, and by adopting or fostering youngsters, they have a ready-made workforce."

Several women of perhaps twenty-five or thirty years of age lined up the children in front of the train. Few were already spoken for, so they were selected in an auction-like event.

"Mr. and Mrs. Kristensen?"

Hazel turned, and her legs trembled. A blonde woman wearing a simple navy-blue dress held the hand of a three-year-old boy with raven-black hair and gray eyes. His round face was punctuated with a tiny dimple in his chin. Thumb in his mouth, he studied them with the seriousness of a court judge.

Olav nodded and extended his hand. "Yes, we're the Kristensens, and this is our daughter, Dagmar, who is very excited at the prospect of a little brother."

The young woman shook his hand and smiled at Hazel and Dagmar. "It is nice to meet all of you. I have the paperwork for your signatures. Is there somewhere private we can complete our transaction?"

"Inside the station may be quieter." He gestured to the low-slung building behind them. "I know the stationmaster. His office may be available."

"Excellent. I'll follow you." She bent and whispered in Henri's ear. He nodded and pulled his thumb from between his lips, waved at them, then tucked the finger back into his mouth.

They marched to the massive building, and Olav led them to the office. As they approached, the door opened, and a beefy man in uniform appeared.

"Just the man I'm looking for," Olav said. "May we borrow your office?"

"Absolutely." The stationmaster's gaze dropped to the little boy. "Is this your new son? You must be excited to welcome him into your family."

"Ja. We've been looking forward to his arrival for weeks."

The man squatted in front of Henri. "Welcome to Green Bay, little man. You're going to be part of the best family in town. You're going to love your new papa and mama."

Henri's eyes darted from the man to Hazel, and after a brief second, a tentative smile curved the youngster's mouth. "Mama?"

Hazel's heart swelled. After months of trying to have a child of their own, she and Olav would finally welcome a new addition to the family. When it seemed she would never get pregnant, they'd reluctantly talked about adoption. But after finding the article about the orphans, they felt God's nudge to grow their family by alternative means. And now their little boy was here.

A wave of nausea swept over her, and she swallowed, pressing a hand against her middle. She needed to see the doctor, but if she wasn't mistaken, God would bless them with another little one in about seven months. Perhaps He'd waited to grant them a child of their union once He saw their willingness to take in a child of their heart. Perhaps not. Whatever His reasons, she was thankful He'd chosen to bless them with siblings for Dagmar.

"Is everything all right?" Concern etched lines in Olav's forehead as he looked at her.

She stroked his jaw, then pulled him close for a kiss. "It couldn't be more perfect. I'm praising God for my family."

"Ja." His eyes sparkled. "He has made my...our lives complete."

Hazel leaned her forehead against his and sighed. Complete, yes. Finished, no.

THE END

What did you think of *A Family for Hazel*?

Thank you so much for purchasing *A Family for Hazel*. You could have selected any number of books to read, but you chose this book.

I hope it added encouragement and exhortation to your life. If so, it would be nice if you could share this book with your family and friends by posting to Facebook (www.facebook.com) and/or Twitter (www.twitter.com).

If you enjoyed this book and found some benefit in reading it, I'd appreciate it if you could take some time to post a review on Amazon, Goodreads, Kobo, Bookbub, GooglePlay, Apple Books, or other book review site of your choice. Your feedback and support will help me to improve my writing craft for future projects and make this book even better.
Thank you again for your purchase.

Blessings,
Linda Shenton Matchett

A Family for Hazel

Did you enjoy this installment of the *Brides of Pelican Rapids* series? Read on for the first chapter of *Vanessa's Replacement Valentine*, another one of Linda's contributions to the series

Chapter One

Pine branches blocked Miles Andersen's vision and scratched his face as he wrestled his end of the massive tree through the front door. His boot caught the threshold, and he stumbled, shoving the mammoth evergreen into his best friend, Henrik Dahl. Miles grimaced. "Sorry, but I told you this thing was too big."

"Nonsense. There's plenty of room in the entranceway. We just have to get it inside and upright." Henrik shifted his grip and grunted. "Almost there."

They eased the conifer the rest of the way into the house and leaned it against the curved staircase. Miles rubbed his hands against his pants, but the patches of sap on his palms remained stuck to his skin. He stepped back and studied the tree. "I must admit, it is magnificent. I'm not sure I have enough decorations to cover it." He tossed a look over his shoulder at Henrik's wife. "What do you think, Rhea?"

She clapped her hands, her face flushed and glowing. "Perfect. If we don't have an adequate amount, I can have the Sunday school children make ornaments. They love to do that." She winked. "In fact, I could bring them here—"

"No, *Lille Julaften* is tonight." He shrugged. "I shouldn't have waited so long to prepare for Little Christmas Eve, but I've had trouble getting into the spirit this year."

Waving a Norwegian flag, she gestured to the evergreen. "Which is why Henrik and I are here. It's difficult to be alone at the holidays, but I'm going to pull out all the stops to give you a proper Christmas season. I'll even make lutefisk if you're extra sweet."

Miles wrinkled his nose. "That's one tradition I can live without, but I appreciate the sentiment. I do look forward to devouring the *pepperkakehaus*. Gingerbread is one of my favorite flavors, and you outdid yourself on this year's house. I believe it's twice as big as any you've ever made."

Her face pinked. "Truth be told, I messed up when combining the ingredients, so I had to double the recipe."

"A happy error." He rubbed his stomach. "I don't know why you're not fat, Henrik, with a wife who cooks as well as Rhea."

"Working the fields, friend. I don't have the luxury of a bunkhouse full of workers like you do. Some of us have to personally work our farms."

Miles forced a smile. He knew Henrik was joking, nonetheless the barb stung. Too many others in their growing town often speculated about his wealth. His hard work had paid off, and he'd slowly acquired several hundred acres of rich farmland that produced good harvests year after year. He didn't take his situation for granted. God had blessed him, but at any time, weather, pests, or some other problem could impact the farm, and he could be destitute. He'd seen it happen to more than a few hardworking men.

The women in Green Bay seemed especially enamored with his financial success. Which was why he was celebrating yet another holiday with his friends rather than a wife. He'd yet to meet a young woman who was interested in him instead of his wallet.

"Your time will come, Henrik. Besides, your lovely bride doesn't seem to mind that you're not rolling in money. Although I'm not sure what she sees in that ugly mug of yours."

Henrik grinned and pecked Rhea on the cheek. "I'm not sure what she sees in me either, but I managed to get her wed before she could change her mind."

"Oh, you two...enough jawing." Rhea rolled her eyes. "Let's put up this tree, so we can begin decorating."

"Let's?" Miles lifted an eyebrow. "Does that mean you're going to help?"

She gave him a cheeky smile. "Yes, I'm going to supervise so you do it correctly."

"Ouch." He wrapped an arm around her shoulders. "Is she always this bossy, Henrik?"

"You have no idea." His friend chuckled. "But I see the glint in her eye, so we'd best get cracking."

With another smile, she crossed her arms and leaned against the wall. "He's learned a lot during our short marriage."

Miles sniffed the air. "And when we're done, we can dig into those *krumkakers* hiding under the towel in that basket."

"So much for sneaking in the treats." She sighed. "Your detecting skills give Sheriff Koetz a run for his money."

"I'll stick to farming, thank you very much." His detecting skills, indeed. He exchanged a glance with Henrik who, unlike Rhea, knew about his spying during the war. Despite the nine years since the conflict ended, his conscience still pricked him when he thought about the deceit and subterfuge he'd used on behalf of the Union. He'd prayed and had endless discussions with God about whether the ends justified the means.

Henrik clapped him on the back. "The sooner we finish the tree, the sooner we can eat."

"Of course." Miles shook his head to clear the somber thoughts cluttering his mind.

Fifteen minutes later, he stood back and admired the towering evergreen while munching on a delicate, curved cookie. "Delicious, Rhea. You've outdone yourself. These are better than my *mamma* used to make."

"Thank you. They're one of my favorites." She winked. "I'll be sure to teach your new wife how to make them."

"What new wife?" He cocked his head as Henrik guffawed across the room.

"The one we're going to find for you."

He held up his hands in surrender. "Good luck with that. The gals in Green Bay seem eager to marry my money but not me. I'm too old to be much of a catch."

"You're not old," she scoffed. "You're *mature*. Besides, at thirty-five, you're the same age as my brother. Any woman would be blessed to have you as her husband. You're a dedicated, gracious man filled with integrity." She cocked her head. "And although not as handsome as my Henrik, you're a good-looking man."

"Kind of you to say, Rhea, but I should probably resign myself to the fact that I'll live out my days alone."

"Nonsense. Tomorrow you and I are going to craft a letter to Ella Milton of the mail-order-bride agency Henrik used to find me. She'll locate the perfect wife for you. Perhaps from down south like me. Even this long after the war, there are girls struggling to find husbands. We lost many boys, and some can't afford to marry and have a family."

Miles gaped at her. A mail-order bride? Was that the answer to finding a wife who would care for him and not his money? "All right, we'll contact this woman, but I don't hold out much hope. And I don't know about getting a Southern bride. I couldn't marry a woman who came from a slave-holding family."

Henrik nudged his shoulder. "You might consider praying about the situation."

Warmth flooded Miles's face. What kind of woman would God send him?

Acknowledgments

Although writing a book is a solitary task, it is not a solitary journey. There have been many who have helped and encouraged me along the way.

My parents, Richard and Jean Shenton, who presented me with my first writing tablet and encouraged me to capture my imagination with words. Thanks, Mom and Dad!

Scribes212 – my ACFW online critique group: Valerie Goree, Marcia Lahti, and the late Loretta Boyett (passed on to Glory, but never forgotten). Without your input, my writing would not be nearly as effective.

Eva Marie Everson – my mentor/instructor with Christian Writers' Guild. You took a timid, untrained student and turned her into a writer. Many thanks!

SincNE, and the folks who coordinate the Crimebake Writing Conference. I have attended many writing conferences, but without a doubt, Crimebake is one of the best. The workshops, seminars, panels, critiques, and every tiny aspect are well-executed, professional, and educational.

Special thanks to Hank Phillippi Ryan, Halle Ephron, and Roberta Isleib for your encouragement and spot-on critiques of my work.

Thanks to my Book Brigade who provide information, encouragement, and support.

Paula Proofreader (https://paulaproofreader.wixsite.com/home): I'm so glad I found you! My work is cleaner because of your eagle eye. Any mistakes are completely mine.

A heartfelt thank you to my brothers, Jack Shenton and Douglas Shenton, and my sister, Susan Shenton Greger for being enthusiastic cheerleaders during my writing journey. Your support means more than you'll know.

My husband, Wes, deserves special kudos for understanding my need to write. Thank you for creating my writing room – it's perfect, and I'm thankful for it every day. Thank you for your willingness to accept a house that's a bit cluttered, laundry that's not always done, and meals on the go. I love you.

And finally, to God be the glory. I thank Him for giving me the gift of writing and the inspiration to tell stories that shine the light on His goodness and mercy.

Other Titles
Romance

Love's Harvest, Wartime Brides, Book 1

Love's Rescue, Wartime Brides, Book 2

Love's Belief, Wartime Brides, Book 3

Love's Allegiance, Wartime Brides, Book 4

Love Found in Sherwood Forest

A Love Not Forgotten

On the Rails

A Doctor in the House

Spies & Sweethearts, Sisters in Service, Book 1

The Mechanic & the MD, Sisters in Service, Book 2

The Widow & the War Correspondent, Sisters in Service, Book 3

Love at First Flight

Multi-author Series

A Bride for Seamus (Proxy Brides, 48)

A Bride for Seamus (Proxy Brides, 62)

Dinah's Dilemma (Westward Home and Hearts Mail-Order Brides, 10)

Rayne's Redemption (Westward Home and Hearts Mail-Order Brides, 15)

Daria's Duke (Westward Home and Hearts Mail-Order Brides, 22)

Legacy of Love (Keepers of the Light, 10)

Vanessa's Replacement Valentine, (Brides of Pelican Rapids, 13)

Gold Rush Bride Hannah (Gold Rush Brides, 1)

Gold Rush Bride Caroline (Gold Rush Brides, 2)

Mystery
Under Fire, Ruth Brown Mystery Series, Book 1

Under Ground, Ruth Brown Mystery Series, Book 2

Under Cover, Ruth Brown Mystery Series, Book 3

Murder of Convenience, Women of Courage, Book 1

Murder at Madison Square Garden, Women of Courage, Book 2

Non-Fiction
WWII Word Find, Volume 1

Biography

Linda Shenton Matchett writes about ordinary people who did extraordinary things in days gone by. She is a volunteer docent and archivist at the Wright Museum of WWII. Born in Baltimore, Maryland, a stone's throw from Fort McHenry, she has lived in historical places most of her life. Now located in central New Hampshire, Linda's favorite activities include exploring historical sites and immersing herself in the imaginary worlds created by other authors.

Website/blog: http://www.LindaShentonMatchett.com
Newsletter signup (receive a free short story):
https://mailchi.mp/74bb7b34c9c2/lindashentonmatchettnewsletter
Facebook: http://www.facebook.com/LindaShentonMatchettAuthor
Pinterest: http://www.pinterest.com/lindasmatchett
Amazon: https://www.amazon.com/Linda-Shenton-Matchett/e/B01DNB54S0
Goodreads: http://www.goodreads.com/author_linda_matchett
Bookbub: http://www.bookbub.com/authors/linda-shenton-matchett

A Family for Hazel